The Last Game We Played

The Last Game We Played

stories

Jo Neace Krause

Black Lawrence Press
New York

Black Lawrence Press
www.blacklawrencepress.com

Black Lawrence Press
8405 Bay Parkway C8
Brooklyn, N.Y. 11214
U.S.A.

Some of the stories in this collection were previously published in the following:
"The Last Game We Played" in *Exquisite Corpse*
"The Whole World Is Watching" in *In Posse Review*
"Blindness" in *River City*
"Things that Make People Unclean" in *Other Voices*
"A Woman In The News" in *The Massachusetts Review*
"The Other Diary" in *Tatlin 's Towers*
"The Good In Men" in *Witness*
"Nothing but Idolatry" in *The Potomac Review*

Published 2008 by Black Lawrence Press, a division of Dzanc Books
Book design by Steven Seighman

Cover image: *Nude in Hat*, by Jo Neace Krause. Permission courtesy of the Kentucky Folk Art Center, Morehead, Kentucky.

First edition 2008
ISBN: 0-9815899-1-6

Printed in the United States

Table of Contents

THE LAST GAME WE PLAYED

"LIKE I SAID, I'M INTO THE GAMES, WAR GAMES FASCINATE me! And after I got laid off from my job at the factory I got into them more. What ya mean, don't ramble? Doctor, you said to drag it out and that's what I'm doing. I can't tell something in just a few words like some of these guys they send up here to you. I'm a talker. Always was. Talkers are gifts to this wretched world, if I must say so myself. And I'm not going to be put down for being what I am. So let me alone. Let me go on with this.

"So I was into the games. I got your guy Seagull into them too. Paul Seagull. The one you want to hang, right? He was a great chess guy. Nothing but chess for him, but then he put that aside after we got forced out of the video plant — that's the factory job I had — and he started coming up to the apartment to play with us. It takes brains to play the way we played. All the military history you've got to memorize. Battles. Battles, backwards and forwards. You should see all the books I've got on just rules alone. Cases of books. Pushed under the beds and all the furniture. You couldn't move in the place for the books.

"So I picked the guys I wanted to play with. Really careful about that. About the people I wanted around me. There were about a dozen of us. All out of work now. We would order the soldiers from this outlet company in Chicago and paint them ourselves. They're like little chessmen. And there's this special paint you buy. You paint them. Slowly. It takes hours. Hours... seems like centuries.

"Not that I'm a purist like some of these guys who once they get into a game have to fix everything just right on a knight's helmet. Just right, you see, or they won't even send him into the lines. I'm not like that. The plumage doesn't matter to me. You can make miniature swords from beer cans. You put your armies on this board, sometimes the size of a pool table. Then you can do anything you want with them because you're the master now. You can let 'em show how history should have happened.

"Paul was great at it, the very best. What a fan, fan, tastic guy! He knew more history, I tell you, than the goddamnn library. Actually, he was a history teacher. He has degrees. College degrees. But he couldn't find a real job. They kept sticking him in these substitute teaching slots. For thirteen years he was a substitute in this run-down neighborhood. Imagine that. The whole school system ran on substitutes. The teachers went to conferences and stayed there. The students seldom saw them. Nobody saw them. They were on paid trips to places like Italy and Indonesia. Improving their minds.

"So he would show us interesting twists on the games we were playing. 'Look here, here is the country's food supply,' he would say, with a map spread out. Look at that supply route. Without this route, New York has about three days' supply of bread. If you blow up this airport, and this one, what do you think is the first thing that's going to happen? Fascinating, huh?

"And when we were still working it was the same. It was Paul who kept things going. You could walk into the factory cafeteria, and there he was in his slouchy clothes, right in the center of the excitement. No one was going to stop him from talking. He was like a vigorous fountain bubbling in the center of this ignorant world. Ranting against the management. Against government. Against everything. How I loved it! Even though he is a Jew, not even Israel escaped a pounding. 'I tried to live there and the atmosphere made me sick,' he said. 'Flag wavers! I hate flag wavers. Always those little blue and white flags with that star on it, stuck right under your nose like somebody's fixed idea of themselves in history. Like living in a football stadium, so I say forget it,' he threw his hand out. 'The end is coming anyway.'

"This was like an explosion in me. I ran after him, cornered him down the hall and asked him what he meant by that. I stood there looking at him, panting, catching my breath. For over a month I had been having bad dreams, scenes of muddy water, so his words meant something. Once I dreamed Hitler called me in to cut his hair. In another I imagined all the houses in town had been swept away in a mudslide and a man was stealing watches and bracelets off the arms of my friends sticking out of the mud. When he saw me looking, he tried to run and fell into the swollen river. I ran along the bank, trying to get him out, watching his terror as the gap widened between his hands and the stick I held down to him. Then he went down. Dreams are omens to me. I feel they reach out of us to the outside, and catch on to little passing remarks, like the one Paul had made.

"He looked at me, wondering, a funny little grin on his lips. We were around the pop machines, which were off in a little dinky leeway like. 'Did I say that?' he asked. He narrowed his eyes, almost amused. 'You really don't know, do you? You really have not seen the danger? Don't you know how everything in this country is getting locked down by these third world pissants? Colonized. Look around you. We're finished.'

"Three days later the plant shut its doors, locked the gates, put guards around. Then I saw how really, really smart he was. How he understood what should have been obvious to me, the way they were getting rid of so many people. Whole departments. 'You mean whole towns,' Paul said, 'whole towns are out of work and nobody is saying anything. Pretending it isn't happening. That's the joke. These big dingy streams of men coming in for their last checks, pretending they have good sense. Sometimes they have on suits. Ha! Finally an occasion to dress up for, right! You oughta see it; it's frightening. The way they push in off the rusting landscape out there and give their name at the desk, always the last name, like it weighs something, carries a big guarantee!'

"'And where the hell are the unions?' he wanted to know. 'Nobody's saying a word. A few demonstrations in places like Gulf Port and Seattle, but that's all. The fact is: they're doing it all on computers, that's the trick. Wasting everybody without even showing their faces. No one in America has a face anymore. The classic American face is a no-face. Big round zero with not even dots for eyes.'

"'It's like a war game,' I said to him, an elation rising in me, as it always does when I can join some idea to a game. 'Because of the silence involved. The terrific silent nakedness of the moves, the quiet cruel violence of the spirit involved. I'm into war games,' I told him. And after awhile he was coming up to see what I was talking about."

"Was it Paul's idea to invite that CEO to the games? Was it perhaps....a game...that just got out of hand?"

"Do you really believe that? Why are they trying to hang something like this on Paul?"

"Did he try it on several other people in your presence? There are your friends who have disappeared, their absences unexplained. Isn't that interesting to you?"

"Do you really believe that story they've got started? That Paul hypnotized the plant CEO and told him to die? And he died! That's the dumbest thing I ever heard! Who on earth would obey such a command? I'm getting scared. Scared of you for thinking something like this. I was hypnotized once. In the sixth grade at school. The hypnotist told me I was a monkey and I leaped all over the balcony and chairs. But to die because someone told me I could set my mind to come back alive in three days and tell everyone about it? No way! Of course, after our arrests by the police, like I told you, I felt something disastrous was about to happen. Some revelation about to be made. I told Judge D'Angelo that, and that's why he said 'I'm not going to send you to jail just now. I'm going to send you to a psychiatrist.' But I know what he really thought. He thought you could get me to dump on Paul. Did Paul invite the CEO up to the games? Ha, that makes me laugh.

"Do you actually think a bunch of factory guys are going to walk up to some rich CEO like that — and one who has just eliminated their jobs to boot...do you think they are going to say, 'Hey, come on up, we 're out of work now, nothing to do but show you a good time.' You think that's going to happen?"

"Well, how did you meet him? If I may be so bold."

"It was like this: an accident. It had to do with an accident. Several of us were down to the lakefront park one day. It was a strange day, almost unreal in its springtime brightness. We wanted to throw a Frisbee around. Catch a few balls. Not a breeze moved anywhere, and then all of a sudden out of nowhere a hell of a storm blew up. And the rain started to pour down in great grey buckets, so that we could hardly see ten yards in front of us. People were running in all directions looking for shelter, and out in the harbor where the storm seemed to be blowing its strongest came the horror of a human voice in distress. The wind fell for a moment and we could see that a sailboat had capsized. That's where the horrible yelling was coming from.

"Immediately Paul took off his shoes and pants and went in after the man and pulled him to safety. I stayed half out of sight, for I was thinking of my dream. The one about the mudslide. It proved again that dreams are warning us. When I finally looked, I saw that the rescued man was... that's right. He was the CEO. The one who had wiped us out of our jobs. He wouldn't let us go, started following us and slapping his hands together, shutting his eyes, and thanking the Lord for Paul. That's how we met him. He and Paul got to talking and one thing led to another. Finally he was coming to the apartment and doing the games. Making little soldiers.

"Turns out the guy is into religion big time. He credited religion with getting him rich. We would listen to him bullshit half the night, about Ronald Reagan saving civilization and all that, but the conversation always got back to religion. To the Jesus thing. I noticed right away how you couldn't keep him away from it.

"'That's because he doesn't believe it. Not down in his soul does he believe,' Paul said one day. And I looked at him in amazement. He looked very strange. Very solemn. Paul sometimes got ferocious migraine headaches that would blind him with light. 'He wants to make a video. He wants to make a video of Christ's last days. Just to see if he can stumble across some way the miracles were faked. And he wants me to show him.'"

"Show him?" I asked. "How show him?"

"Like I say, by acting through the Jesus story, to get the feel of what might have really, really happened."

"What did Paul know of the Bible?"

"What did Paul know of the Bible! His mind was all over it like a scanner. He knew the Bible backwards and forwards. Like it had something to say. He could quote you scripture and verse in his sleep. Turns out the CEO is ready to put up big money for the video. He is very serious about it, and equally serious about keeping every penny accounted for. His name was Gurney. Burt Gurney. But you know that — what am I thinking about? The deceased. This head of Crux Video. Gurney boy. Well, he could be a nasty, I tell you. Like the day he asked me, 'How old are you?'. 'Twenty,' I said quickly. He looked at me a long time, then back down at his game. 'If a man is not something by the time he is twenty, he will never be something,' he declared. And then he'd say other peculiar things. Like 'Money doesn't matter. It's not worth a hair on my head.' But if you reached for a quarter on the table his fist would close over it like a cat over a bird. And if he brought a little something over to the apartment for us to eat, like lunch meat, or some dip, he'd stare at you every time you took some. He was very skinny himself. I never saw him eat.

"But we began to lay plans for the big game. We started right off, improvising. Making little Jesus and disciple dolls and putting them on the board. Making up the dialogue as we went. The video was to be divided into several parts. The Street Preaching. The Arrest. The Crucifixion. And then the Resurrection. Gurney himself played Jesus. He was very good at it, like he had stepped out of the inflamed core of those times. He loved it. He began to let his hair grow long, his face pale. He was a mess, but what could you say, it was his money.

"Everything was going along just great. And yet I had this feeling. It was on me again, this heaviness, like we were living in the last days. A depression came on me. I would sleep for days. Then I would change and be just the opposite, other way around, a fine sharp trembling joy would seize me, travel up and down my body like little teeth pretending to eat my flesh.

"One morning I felt especially wonderful, and ran into the bathroom, ripped the blinds off the windows and began to shower and sing in the golden light, throwing water all over my head and shaking my hair as if to get rid of the meaningless of the life I had led up to this point. A baptism, if you like. I was ready for something big. Big. But when I'm like this, I tell you, any little thing can throw me off. Like the phone call I got from my former wife. She suspected something.

"Word somehow reached her that I wasn't exactly starving, and here she wants to come. Smelling the dollar bills. She had been in Tennessee. Up there singing her distress bullshit songs in some survival tearoom in Memphis. And always after me, all the time to send her money, more money for clothes or she'd have the Family Law after me for failure to support. Threatening to swear out warrants that I was using drugs and anything else she could think up. I had no time for her and her arguments. The morning I got the call she was already here in town. 'You said you would write when you found work. Why did you lie to me?'

"I invited her up to the apartment. My first intentions were to slap the piss out of her so she would leave me the hell alone."

"It says here in the police report that you actually tried to push your former wife, Ms. Goletta's head down in an aquarium. That's a serious charge."

"Doctor, we're living in serious times. And I take our time serious. The aquarium was on the table being used as the Dead Sea. I had the multitudes around it while I made up my lines. I was showing her what we were doing. I tried to make her see the violence in the air. She had just asked me, 'Where have you been? What have you been doing?' That's when I grabbed her hand. And she was suddenly terrified. Real sorry she had ever come to pester me. 'Where have I been! Why, I've been to First Century Jerusalem. That's where. With all my friends. That's where! And, and for a bunch who wanted to change the world we couldn't have found a better place. The air there was wild,' I told her. 'Everyone out of work, but crazy with ideas. So, yes, yes, let me tell you where I've been!' I said, grinding my teeth in her face.

"I showed her the board where we had all the players carved and painted. I raked my finger through the dust on the wood. 'These are the roads, the dusty Galilee countryside where rumors flew about the crucifixion, and where more stoning of the Roman legions were taking place. More cleansing of Zion's soil.' I showed her what the multitudes looked like — they looked desperate, hungry, all painted various hues of grey and dull browns. Even the women were colorless. Color wasn't invented when you looked at these women. You could imagine them, screaming to have devils cast out and the like. Throwing themselves in the roads. But the Nazarenes, these trashy Nazarenes who were causing all the trouble and surprising everyone with their sudden drawing power with the crowds, these were painted a bright cobalt blue.

"'All day long,' I told her, 'we had been around the shores, drying our nets and selling a little fish. Sometimes we heckled the miracle workers, threw stones or just roughed up the dwarfs and cripples. What did we care, wasn't time running out? Wasn't the end near? And here, here comes the trashball Nazarenes again.' I walked them around on the table, making a whizzing noise with my tongue. 'They are despised everywhere for their diseased meekness and crackpot ideas, but now they claim they are going to prove they can put a man up on the cross and bring him down again and he will still live.'

"'It is a dumb argument but one that is beginning to polarize the entire countryside. There is talk about a new army on the way from Rome to put down any revolt that might be growing. From the rooftops of the town you can watch the new reinforcements the emperor is sending in. They are three or four inches high. Painted either a vivid red or gold. With perfect plumage on the helmets. Marching on foot. Their armor and feet flashing together in the sun and descending into the wider public square where the women start the jeering and insults as soon as the first soldier struts into view around the corner.' I made her see that. I took some of the soldiers and made them run across the edge of the table. I made her shut her eyes and see it.

"'And now the scene we had been waiting for,' I announced loudly, right next to her ear. 'The appearance of their teacher. They began bringing him in. The one they said they were going to put up, let die, then bring back to life. There was a lot of commotion. Five or six guys on either side of him. They would be a little arrogant, as if they were seeing into a mirror dangling the future before them. Then there is this man who stepped out of the crowd and began yelling something. "We've been kept guessing too long about this thing called death! You said you could kill him and bring him back to life, so let's see you do it!"'

"In the video we would change a few things. They would be messing and combing his hair. My fingers moved around in the box until I found what I wanted: the Jesus image Paul had made. It astonished me with its craftsmanship and magic. It was as if I were seeing the teacher for the first time myself. Paul had done such an excellent job on him. I remember how Gurney had gone pale on seeing it too. He reached his fingers to touch him, the long red hair and white limbs, and Gurney's eyes glowed like he had a fever.

"You think of him yourself. The way he ended up against the sky, his long slender legs so beautiful and white out of the tragedy that seems to hang over the centuries in some strange, exhausted, and haunting wonder.

"So they took him and killed him while we watched. Yet he had not bled when that spear lanced his side. Paul kept jabbing me with his elbow to draw this to my attention. No blood, that was the main thing we noticed. That was the big tip-off. I told my wife every little thing. Her eyes were enormous, ready to fill up with hysteria. So we kept watching. Standing there among the multitudes with everyone drawn back in awe when the sky grew black, and saying it was the power of the heaven.

"But it seemed to us as if his body were on hold. As if his life had retreated to a depth where death could not reach it, and there waited, in a kind of sleep. We kept talking about it. Especially Paul, who never wavered in his belief that some rational explanation was possible. And he was persistent. He couldn't rest in his wondering. *What do you think happened? Really happened?* He kept asking this one question. My former wife had relaxed somewhat now and was listening very closely. Not trying to run for the door. How had they done it? How?

"For here was the teacher, alive again. We made him tall and almost lifelike for her. I walked him along the sea, along the aquarium where he performed his magic tricks. I turned on a small fan so his robes would move as if a sea wind were blowing them . Clean blowing robes that the women had brought him. 'We got the answer. We found it,' I told her now, 'Yes, yes, yes!'

"We got it from a disciple. I showed her the disciple, represented by a dehydrated rat I had taken from a trap in the back hallway. Dehydrated rats last forever. I don't know why. Anyway I made a little robe for him. They could sew in Biblical times. They had needles. Easier for a camel to go through the eye of a needle than for a rich man to get into heaven. Ha, Gurney hated to hear that! Anyway this certain disciple had a weakness in him for drink, and we took him and coaxed him to the house of a whore. Whore? Think Fat Doll. Garbage dumpsters are full of dolls. I could take my pick.

"So the whore was a fat one and wore a cheap heraldic cross around her neck. She claimed to be one of the teacher's first converts. Finally the disciple got full enough and talked. Everyone knew he was not on equal footing with the others but wanted to spill the secret, to get even somehow. He felt very important with his head in the whore's lap and a drink in hand.

"It was very simple, this disciple told her. It was the passionate blood-sweating praying. It put him in a trance. In the garden he prayed all night, repeating the same words until he hypnotized himself, then when the time came, he willed himself dead — with the understanding that he would wake up again in three days. After that Paul was beside him. How could he put this in his video? How? But he wasn't looking around for someone to try it out on, no sir. He knew it was hopeless. My wife is crazy for saying we tried this out on Gurney.

"I even took her across the hallway to meet Paul and the others. I knew Gurney was there, too. He was sleeping in a chair, sound asleep. He had been working very, very hard. If I knew he were dead, why would I take her over to meet him...who would want to introduce someone to a dead person?"

"But it says here in the statement your former wife gave to the police: 'My ex-husband made me go across the hallway. When we opened the door the thick smell of the dead man hit me so hard it was like a putrid ocean in my face, and I started screaming and vomiting. My ex was shouting something at me, something like it's the greatest miracle ever told! I don't know where my strength came from, but I tore away from him and somehow got out of that building. I ran into the street screaming for help and collapsed.'"

"So what? Like I say, Gurney must have had a heart attack! You can't prove otherwise. I don't care, I know you can't!"

"Heart attack! Why didn't you tell someone? He had been dead three days. You people must have been sitting there waiting. Waiting there, waiting for him to come back to life, weren't you! My God, in all my born days as a forensic psychiatrist! Is any of this real?"

"I'm not going to tell you anything else."

A Woman in the News

GOOD EVENING. LET ME BEGIN THIS CLASS WITH THE SAME MESSAGE I give all my students in the theater: If the most important thing in your life right now is not acting, then you've got no business in this room tonight. I mean that. If you are in here for mere entertainment, you might as well get up and go back out the door and find something else to do. I want no one in here robbing my program of its seriousness. I'll find you out if you're not serious.

And I'll send you away to do something else, perhaps to open up a little restaurant somewhere. Nothing wrong in that. Restaurants are every artist's other dream. Like with Kafka. All Kafka ever wanted according to his own words was to open up some little cubbyhole off the sidewalks in Tel Aviv where he could pour tea and listen to chitchat flowing all day like a dream. He even had the tablecloths picked out. Blue and white. He ironed those tablecloths in his sleep. Folded them neatly, spread them in the sun. Bowed to his first customer.

So! So if you don't have that red hot ball burning in the center of your brain for the theater, then please go out and find your own little drama with tablecloths and make yourself cheerful pouring cognac and Colt 45 to your audience.

Well, I shall wait a second. I'll just walk up and down here before you. Waiting for those who are not really determined, to stir themselves and leave us in peace.

Ah, no one moves. No sound of any boots except my own. Good. That's fine. I think we can go on. Understand I am not here simply to strut my stuff, great reputation as a methods teacher that I am. I am here to locate that hidden force inside each of you, the one that does not stop at your last breath but keeps on going until you let that other self out...the self you will be doing in front the class when I call on you. I want you to walk up here as one person, but someone else must walk back in your shoes and take your seat. Understand? Let us begin.

You. You there in the back of the room. Yes, you. In the blue blouse. You first. I want you to come up here and do someone. Do someone in the news. Say, let's see. The woman who has been all over the news saying she didn't kill her child. That West Virginia woman. Yes. Patsy Ramsey. Clearly a woman in crisis, struggling before the cold judgment of her countrymen. Imagine the inward horror and inward pride of standing up and facing down millions of people who want only to hang you. The perfect terror for locating something within yourself. So go ahead now, bring on the magic.

Yes. Go ahead. Just come up here. Take out your comb and fluff out your hair a little. Bend forward on the stool and cover your face for a minute to think about her. You can take on her face, you know — all faces are breakable molds, just abstract forms of character, all its failures and hardship are in it. All its little victories as well, shifting and floating in the eyes like sunshine on the surface of a river. And that iron will which makes room for the smile no matter how it hurts. And the soft lies, the affected flow of truth. All these a good actress will let rise into contact with an audience, the tensions and fears and conceits, those central portions of the character that must burn and dim and glow and blind.

Touch your face. Feel it!

People touch their faces for a reason. Remember that. They run their fingers over their temples, toy with their hair, bite their lips, stare dazed and transfixed. All little spasms of ego protection. But think how Patsy let her hands lie quietly in her lap. She's a hard study in a way. But let's see how you do. Take the stool and sit on it in the middle of the room under the spot light. Just dim the light a little over there for her! Fine! Fine! Now speak! Say a few words. Don't' be afraid.

I'm not afraid. I may look afraid, but I am not!

I am before the world and I am not afraid.

The cameras are up in my face.

That's good. Go on.

I'm not afraid.

I pointed my finger at the murderer. I looked beyond the camera, straight at him with a full stare that seemed only a few feet away from him, as if I were taking everything in, registering his nervousness, his head turning away. I could almost feel him detach himself in a snort of cold anger, pulling away as I pointed my finger. You know who you are! I said.

You know and God knows!

I spoke with directness, trying to make the full force of my bitterness show in that lighted-up meatyard of a place where I had been thrown. But I don't think I was successful. I was trying too hard.

Good. Really good. Go ahead. Then what?

Well, someone said of that interview...the one in which we declared our innocence...they said your husband and you were not touching. Your husband did not take your hand to console you. You looked estranged from each other. Alone. Out there alone before the world. Alone! But let me tell you this: Death estranges people.

That's true. Go on.

When someone dies, when someone is snatched away from you, do you actually think you are going to be full of love for this world? For anyone? When you have been defrauded by a criminal? When your arms and insides are empty? And all life lingers in a smoldering, hateful anger like a hammer has come down on you? Just think how you push people away for almost nothing. Like when you hurt your little finger you scream, *get away from me, leave me alone!* So think what you would do if a hammer hit your whole body. That's something hard to imagine.

Hard to imagine the pain. Pain like blood oozing out from under a hammer.

Then one day, just as you have given yourself over to the pain and lie like some half-devoured rodent in the jaws of a snake...just then you realize something has happened. Like it might be all right, like with a bad headache when you realize that while the pain is not going away, it isn't getting any worse either. And this dim realization, this small hope, is even better for you than when the headache actually does go away.

Yet I don't think people are ready to let me get well. It is frightening to see how their imaginations soar and beat at the windows of our life, wanting in, like flocks of bloodthirsty hungry birds following some wounded animal. In restaurants, eyes seek me out — you can tell who leads the bitter, spiteful little lives — how their eyes seek out my eyes for just one brief exchange of revenge.

Even my next-door neighbor, a woman who burdened me for years with her petty personal problems, opened her door and shouted, *don't try to come in here!* As if I ever wanted to see her sour, bunched-up face in close quarters. People call us and say horrible things. They say, I know exactly how you did it. My own father did that to me. My mother put a plastic thing inside me. She held my legs back over my shoulders. Shut up, she said. You don't know what's good for you.

People actually say brutal things like that — as if we are one of their own secret demons come to life before them in the flesh, demons they can openly address — or one of their evil relatives and to punish us is to set their own lives straight, so with a clean slate and heart they can go on, enter into charities and philanthropic work. I never expected any of this!

What did people do to cleanse themselves before we came along? That's what I want to know. It's really very funny. Some of the hideous mail we get: *Sometimes I would like to take me a pussy and shave ever bit of the hair right off it.* They actually write letters like that. Dangerous letters.

Everyone around us is dangerous. I'm frightened of everyone. We moved several times, spent a long time finding this last place we have settled into. About five miles from where we now sit. We thought the high bluffs above it and the lake in front with its windy rocky beaches would protect us from the crowds, but nothing stops them. Not even the stormy winds that rush straight in off the water serves as a buffer zone against their intrusions. You can smell the police and media everywhere. It is impossible to tell one from the other, cops and reporters. They're the same type, these cops and reporters — working together, partying together, laughing and drinking, and who knows what-all. Playing guitars and building fires, getting tanked up before they start circling our grounds, cameras and recorders in hand, breaking twigs with their tedious stepping drunk feet outside the windows, tripping the security wires so that the lights go on all over the house at all hours and alarms scream out like the death squad is lining you up, coming on the stairs, shouting your name. I come awake with my bare feet running somewhere on a strange floor, not yet carpeted, unfamiliar and cold like stone.

I run room to room in the bright glare of the lights, searching for my family. Sobbing to find my husband who is always awake and never shows fear. He is strangely indifferent to the crying alarms when I find him down the hall in his own room. He has his own bedroom since it is impossible to rest around me. I sweat in my sleep, toss and turn since going off the estrogen. He can't stand my restlessness, my nightgown drenched with perspiration.

My husband stands quietly, his head sideways, listening, looking away from me. He is dressed in a bathrobe, terrycloth, white. But under the robe he is wearing jeans and a shirt, just in case. We are silent for an hour, maybe two, after the alarm and lights go back off automatically, just lying there feeling the dark pressing into us, silencing us. We lie like two ties on a railroad track with a long, long train going across.

What day is it? I ask my husband. I can't remember the days anymore. I haven't slept in months. Repeated dreams of water dripping somewhere. In a dark basement, a dog yelping in violent pain, screaming with horror. I sit in the kitchen waiting for the water to boil, groggy and brooding. Alone in the early morning. Fog bank over the lake. Yet aware of feet, thousands of feet, a formless tide of sneakers, sandals, racing athletic feet, leaping around the windows, keeping time faster and faster. I jump up, and in one angry step jerk open the door so the blinds and curtains swing in a swishing rattle. This causes panic in the spying creatures who run and jump off the porch with a scream, and hide in the shrubbery. I can hear a young girl's scolding voice. Blaming her companion. *Lisa, you queer! You blew it! Shut up, there she is. She's sticking her head out the door. Run! Run!* I can see their backs running, just high school kids in bright red and blue jackets, the bushes and grass parting for their bodies quick as wild rabbits.

One of them, a pretty blonde, has been here before, hanging around with her boyfriend, who is dressed in mission clothes, carrying a battered-up guitar. Slumming for the summer. All day I can see them walking around, sometimes far out on a knotty backbone of rocks scaring the sky out of the lake. We have a television in the kitchen. A very small one, no bigger than a slice of toast, but still capable of pulling in the world with its great, laughing, accusing crowds that must be fed hourly, on the hour, never changing, like a miserable imbecile that stays the same forever. But this news is old, a month old. It's about us.

It is about us moving. On the move, trying to get away, but identified by our furniture which is being stacked in a loading van. A naked mattress hoisted in the air and trotted about, exposed to the world a month ago, but still being looked at, stared at in re-runs. Strangers letting their minds climb on it, this personal blue mattress, climbing into our arguments, settling everything for us, as we lie there, two heads, two telephones, talking and talking, to lawyers, to doctors, to friends, our necks bent, our elbows raw, talking, talking until I simply cannot utter another sound that would be considered human. Nothing. My tongue has fallen back in my throat, swollen, paralyzed. We made love once after her death. Then we turned away from each other, that one healing denied us: for some hidden reason we didn't want each other again.

Remember what I told you about the face. Concentrate on the face.

Unlike most women, I don't stand in the bathroom and study my face. It is impossible to know your own face, which is an abstract form of character...just like you said... failure and hardship and love. If I had to draw my face I could not do it. Where to start? Once I saw my face as an abstract form of success. A physical success. Because I had won a state-wide beauty contest. But it was hard to recognize that face in the photographs as my own. Yet it was mine. I owned it. The instant I heard my name called out I drew in my breath as someone else. I could feel my face change and rise out of the old me and into a realm of chosen beauty, glistening in the bursting thunderstorm of acceptance, like a live sparkler thrown up against the dark sky at night. Once I had won, you see, no one could argue about my being beautiful. It's a look you get then. Like the way a rich person's face looks rich.

Maybe you don't know what I am talking about. Maybe it dumbfounds you to be told what I know: that it is possible to construct yourself out of one grand bursting moment of admiration. But I believe that, just as I believe it is possible to become ugly if the world declares you ugly. Think of it this way: before I won the prize I was just somebody who was rather pretty, and I think people were blind to me the way they are blind to most things about them that doesn't get up in their faces.

That's what being beautiful is, getting up in the face with your act. Like Marilyn Monroe. I never thought she had anything, but there she was, an act of beauty. Acting. I used to go to work, ride the bus downtown and no one would notice me. I had gotten out of bed, stuck on some lipstick and high heel shoes, went trudging off. Ha, like I say, I hadn't happened.

Then I won a state-wide contest. Months later in the blank silence of my parents' house I would re-run the video film of my being crowned. They had given the film to me as a present, and I sat in the dark and watched it, flushed and alone, in a kind of frenzy as the glittering crown came down on my head with the other contestants running up to me, covering me with their tears, with their smiles, touching me with their hands of love. I sat in the dark watching some woman who said she was me, who had risen from me; a woman they said was beautiful, weeping from the joy of being beautiful. What this meant for me and my future need not be guessed at any longer.

A year later I was married to a man I could not have otherwise met. A man who would not have otherwise found me attractive. I am convinced of that. He laughs at me when I say this, his eyes gleaming over the top of his glasses. But I had been declared beautiful and this made him see something beyond his own eyes.

O.K. Now the wedding. Do you want me to lead you through the wedding?

Just tell what it meant.

It meant that beauty had won again. That a beautiful face stands in defiance against the travail of existence. Against all bad news in the world. And the wedding itself, that ceremonial beauty of love, that theater of the heart. Like everyone else here in this room, I can't live without it, that love...that beauty.

It was a beautiful woman's wedding. Rather solemn and subdued, with Bach's *Toccata and Fugue in D Minor* filling the vaunted ceiling of the church, and later, when I and my attendants came down the church steps in our floating satin and flowers, the air was full of splendid bells carrying like a cold thrill in the air over that breezy old mountain river town where I grew up in West Virginia.

Beauty like that could win against everything, all unhappiness.

You mean you were not happy? Was there some change you felt later? What?

Oh, I was amazingly happy. So many wonderful friends. We traveled a great deal, mostly in connection with my husband's business. Then there was the month I discovered I was having the little girl they say we murdered. I can't say her name. Sorry. Sorry. Sorry. It hurts me so! Forgive me! Well, at first I was ecstatic, I never looked more beautiful. Everyone was telling me how I seemed to be awakening, growing more radiant in my own secret warmth. But there was something else. Something they didn't know about.

At times a black tidal wave of depression swept over me. A wave of boredom mixed with no will to push it away. That's the way I felt. The doctor caused it! This doctor who was supposed to take care of me!

When I went in for the first checkup I had this strange feeling about him. That he resented me. As a woman. That he did not like women, and perhaps saw pregnancy as a payback for all the admiration they had received from the world, all the applause that lead up to a marriage. Yes, he seemed to get a kick of seeing women trapped. Don't look at me like people aren't like that! I could feel it...I changed doctors...but wouldn't you know when the time came for my delivery, my own doctor was not in the hospital. He could not be located, but this doctor I had discharged was on duty. He looked at me and smiled, but when we were alone he said something like *you better keep your ass down on the table.*

Then the baby came and I forgot all about him. Forgot everything except the beautiful baby who took up most of my thinking and most of my heart. No one seemed able to mention her without some passionate adjective attached to her. *How is the little princess? Our little heart-breaker?* and so forth, as if she were an on-going project in the stock market. How's the princess stock doing? Up again, huh? Wonderful!

So I knew something about beauty. Beauty is like intelligence. Like a high I.Q. It's just a potential. And a potential can be passed over, like a winning ticket in a blind man's pocket. It is something you must bring out before the world and keep it there, or it will be lost forever.

That's why we competed in all those contests for beautiful children. It took up a great deal of our time, of course, and there was the jealousy we had to face, the malicious envy that rose in the other mothers. We had to be very careful when we won. Not to look too happy, but to stick a kind of non-living, beaming smile to our faces that women do who know the losers are watching.

Oh, I knew. I knew what kind of resentment and dangerous feelings she stirred up in others.

The way their eyes narrowed looking at her, my daughter who was so natural a heroine she did not even have to exert herself before the camera. She knew who the camera loved to touch. You've seen that face. I don't have to tell you anything. But I couldn't understand all this luck I had. Having a daughter like this. It was like waking up and finding some bright jeweled watch ticking in your ear at the end of a cloudy dream.

Therefore I was baffled when the depression came back, that shadowy misery I just told you about...that flattish, provoking impatience. I realized after awhile it had to do with the way my daughter's life was at a standstill. Nothing was moving. All those little shows that had once excited us so much, that kept me awake at nights, rushing here and there, fighting with seamstresses. Yes, seamstresses! Like that old crazy Mrs. Kabough, a religious fanatic. Bony white face, very white bushy hair all around her head. Wouldn't sew a stitch on a costume if it wasn't to be used in a Christian pageant. Had to keep telling her lies. She's going to be one of the angels that overlook the little baby Jesus. It's for the Christmas show, Mrs. Kabough. At the Presbyterian Church. No, there is no dancing. No, no paint on her face.

So we did the shows. Over and over. But it was like seeing a movie you loved over and over again and expecting something to come of it. Some change. Like seeing *National Velvet* over and over and feeling that something will come to you too, some marvel, some big win. But nothing ever did. That's the only way I can explain my suffocation.

And all those people we were meeting. What good was that? Look at all the people the Queen of England meets, all the hands she shakes, all the talk, talk, talk. What good does that do her? What can she do now that she couldn't do when she was fifteen years old? That was the way I was thinking. And the videos. The hundreds of videos which I sent off packed in special wooden crates. Insured for thousands of dollars. Off to all the famous studios. I was sure they would be receptive. But no agent called us. I wrote letters and always received a form to fill out with a donation fee to be included. I desperately wanted to see my daughter do certain famous movies. *National Velvet. The Wizard of Oz*. Or perhaps movies I might even write myself. Especially for her.

The writing idea was now a very important dream for me. Because the world was cooling off to me. As a woman. I was approaching that age when a woman begins to disappear. No one sees you any longer, it is as if you are actually disappearing — existing as a shadow, a dim faded form, something people do not really consider a presence. I was down. Hurting. Perhaps hurting. Was I really hurting?

I don't know. I'm not sure. I could not tell if it was actual pain or just hunger. A malignant sort of hunger. Where you have to eat all the time. I don't know. I only know that I deserted my friends a lot. Women I swam with, had those pool parties with children.

Often I went off alone. I strolled downtown. Explored the parks. The smoky grease smells of a dirty little food vendor drew me through the trees. I would go there about eleven o'clock each day. To sit on the benches, watch people strolling about.

Near this one place where I liked to go by myself, there were shops and tanning parlors. Exercise rooms. One such exercise room opened directly on to the sidewalk with an expansive window where you could see a crowd of men inside dressed in sweats and muscle shirts. They would be riding the machines and equipment like a herd of stallions, lifting weights, walking treadmills, doing things that would make a new person out of an old one.

I began to watch a man just inside the window. He was wearing baggy shorts and riding a stationary bike. It annoyed him to be stared at, so he began to pedal very rapidly as if trying to get away from me, my stare. His color reddened, darkened. But of course he could not get away from my eyes. And this made me smile. I was very amused watching a man trying to pedal away in a window. I began to smile even more until finally we both broke out in a laugh. Then I walked away. I was sorry I had disturbed him. I walked away and I didn't come back to the park for a whole week.

When I did, when he saw me this time, he grabbed his shirt and came outside and stared at me the way I had stared at him. He stared very intently, aggressively, as if he were holding my arm, my wrist, not exactly friendly, not unfriendly. Not angry either, but straining, as if it could go either way, depending on my next move. I told him my name and he said, *Patsy*. Patsy. Like he was tasting a new drink or something.

I was surprised to hear his accent. It sounded southern, maybe Appalachian. But the look wasn't Appalachian. Appalachians have their own look. You know it if you come from there. A worn-down look. This man had a vigorous quality as if his life had been preserved by order and knowledge of how to work without hurting yourself. He was on the short side. Short guys...that's the best kind there is, he said. Only his teeth made him look rough. One tooth was broken, chipped. Good-looking. Dark. Studying me intently, trying to find out if I was interesting. He stood with his jacket over his arm, staring at me, studying my face. One day we will have to help each other die.

Again I walked away and left him staring after me. He didn't try to stop me. I kept thinking about him. Then one afternoon the phone rang and I heard his voice. It's me — from the gym. There was a long silence. Then he said, *I think you know what I want.*

My heart began to really pound. It was very exciting. No one had paid attention to me like this in a long time. I didn't know exactly how to act. I really didn't. Should I run down there right then? Or what? I'm planning to come tomorrow, I told him. But please, don't call here anymore. Later when I got to know him I told him right out: if you want to see me you've got to know how to keep your mouth shut.

No problem, he said quietly.

At times he was very quiet, silent.

After one of his long silences he put his arm around me and said,we're going to do something really bold to get your daughter noticed. We're going to bypass all the usual marketing schemes. Go for something really bold. The world will belong to her after all, I promise you.

He began to tell me his plan. It was simple-minded and childish. I was indifferent. I let it roll in my head like a wheel as he kissed my throbbing throat, my face, made love to me. I half-listened, languid and eager for his fine body. I had driven all that way down there, through all that traffic, and I wanted my orgasm.

Sometimes I didn't hear from him for days. I was writing. I wrote. Or tried to write. I thought up plots that might please the popular mind. It's no secret. The notebooks are in the hands of the police. They have gone over them and checked them out, disappointed no doubt that they are fiction. Untrue. Not the truth. All made-up stuff. Then she was dead. Then we were accused. My life whirled away from me in a roar.

Out of this roar rushed all these yelling people. We walked through them with our attorney by our side. He was a good friend and, along with our other friends, behaved as if something were about to be taken away from them, too — personally, illegally, and they must stop it with their knowledge and expertise. Their money and words. My attorney is very combative, very expensive. I can tell you one thing about him. No one has ever got the best of him, inside a court house or outside of it.

Don't be frightened, he told me, *answer everything straight out. They're keeping us waiting on purpose here. To humble us. But we won't be humbled.* He was looking very closely at me. *They're just cops. A bunch of showboats. They'll mess it all up in ten minutes. All we have to do is wait.*

PART II

The detectives came in groups of threes. Three men in suits on each side of the table. Six men.

Then two women joined them, followed by a staff of assistants. So the room was now crowded with people who talked briskly among themselves, ignoring us altogether. They had brought in a lot of equipment with them and some technicians were fooling with it. Recorders and laptop computers. When they were finished setting it all up, my lawyer rose and, with his big steps, went around the table, objecting. Michael, it was understood that this was not a deposition. No sworn statements and no recordings. I thought you understood that. You don't have the authority to record my client. His hair had just been cut and it stood up shiny with gel, like a rooster's comb. A fighting cock. He kept running his hand under his belt and stopping with his legs apart, objecting to everything.

But it turned out the recording equipment was for another party. It had nothing to do with me. In fact, we were asked to move to another room altogether, a smaller one that looked like someone's kitchen with a stainless steel sink and coffee maker. It seemed to have been used recently by someone who had washed their hands and dried them quickly. I noticed a paper towel lay crumbled and wet on the counter. The detectives were all well dressed and groomed. Rather young. Much younger than my husband, who sat with his head to the side as if he were thinking about something in another city. He did not look at me.

The interrogator was soft-spoken once we began, very polite. He made me feel almost relaxed, even among friends.

Then he did something that disturbed me. He unexpectedly looked me straight in the eyes. For one assaulting second.

I stared back defiantly, unblinking, surrendering nothing. I shook his eyes off me . I felt no one could approach me with a look like that. My good clothes would keep them back. I was wearing a blue suit with a flash of white trim that might suggest piety and strength at the same time, the white of a priest's collar, the blue of a woman's navy uniform. Good shoes and purse. Earrings like two elongated tear drops. But I never reached up nervously and touched them.

Spread before the detectives on the table were my notebooks, diaries, material from a fiction writing class I had been taking at the community college, a night class. The police confiscated these from my property. Everything was numbered and tagged. Each time the detective picked up a scrap he read off a number to a woman assistant who wrote it down. *What is B.T.'s full name? This boyfriend of yours?*

She has no boyfriend. She's already answered that question a dozen times, my attorney shot back, while I sat perfectly unmoved. *She has no boyfriend and had none. It's made-up stuff for a fiction class. We've told you that.*

The detective kept his eyes on me, waiting for me to speak. It's true. I write stuff. I want to publish one day. Something for the popular mind. Find a publisher. An editor.

And this. You wrote this. Met with B.T. at hotel today. He had never been in a place this exclusive. He was very impressed, proud to be with me. He ran out for ice. I let him know I was disappointed, however, in his going back on cigarettes. But he said, *I'm learning. You quit and quit until you learn how to quit.* But I didn't like someone smoking and then trying to kiss me. I told him. He kept talking about the plan but I wanted what I wanted when I wanted it. I had to have my satisfaction. After all, I had driven all the way down there, through all that traffic.

And here you continue. Item number three, page twenty-five of your notebook. It's just a look he has. Knowing. Cunning. Very exciting. I told him I liked his rough smile and he said thanks. But these two teeth here on the bottom are false, he said, tapping on them with his finger. And what about you, Patsy-girl? You got anything in your head that's false?

Item number thirty-four of the notebook. He already knew everything about my daughter. He has seen her pictures. But now I started bringing movies of her to the room where we met when my husband was out of town. Showed him how she took over the camera like she was kicking the world out of her way. I told him at one time I believed she would be discovered the way I had been discovered: in a sudden moment.

Item number thirty-five. B.T. is not you usual biker type. But once was in a biker gang called The Huck Loves. The name Huck Love written on his shoulder blade. Not a hood type. In fact, went two years to law school. Dropped out. Drugs? Can't tell. His nerves are sometimes jumpy.

What's B.T.'s full name? This Huck Love guy you were laying around with?

Really, Mike! She doesn't have a boyfriend! She's already told you that five times. My lawyer shot out while I sat perfectly unmoved.

That blue suit I had on is a favorite of mine. The earrings, like two tear drops, were a present from my husband. *She has no boyfriend and had none. Who in God's name ever heard of The Huck Loves? I never heard of any such group. For Christ's sake, it's made-up stuff for a fiction class. We've been all over that like a plague.*

The detective kept his eyes on me, waiting for me to speak. It's true, I said. It's all made-up stuff. Like I said, I write stuff. I want to publish one day. Something for the popular mind. Find a publisher.

And this B.T. is rough, but not your real live bad guy type. Not sleazy. Very animated after watching the movies of her. We watched them over and over. When I left I asked for his shirt. Shirt off his back. I began pulling it over his head, acting silly. And now I bury my face in its smell like old leather and sweat until I find myself breaking down in tears. O.K. Who is this man that made you break into tears?

Doesn't exist. I told him. I had to make him up. Like most women do.

I hate the way the detective stares at me in disbelief. Like I'm lying. Protecting a murderer. He is older than he looked at first. His hands tremble slightly.

And this, he continues, reading from my notes. I was very excited about having my life taken seriously again. Having someone who would listen to me and let me explain myself. My dreams that were so faraway. My daughter's dreams.

It means nothing, I told him softly, not in the least embarrassed. I was trying to form a plot. Just get something down on paper. For a class. I take writing classes. And acting lessons. I took a handkerchief out of my purse and dabbed at my forehead with it. Then I looked into the handkerchief with a little anxiety, as if I expected to see blood. My heart had begun to pound. Just something I scribbled. I usually burn my stuff. My poetry. I burned it all up. You've seen the last of my writing, I told him, as if hurt by his attitude.

My client's desires to be a writer are well known, my attorney said again with a sort of deadness. *And an actress.*

You. You, the detective says to me. During one of your meetings with this B.T. guy that you had been laying around with...This Huck Love. Around Christmas. You told him about the Christmas party you and your husband were going to? You said it would be a good time to execute the kidnapping scheme, right?

No. I never knew anyone by that name.

Michael is a tall, grey-haired detective with a face permanently distorted by suspicion, with that certain braced coldness for the world people in his job of investigations take on after awhile, fixing to their life a calculated, unfeeling insight into the human race. He kept looking directly into my eyes as we talked, slowly playing with a pencil. We talked a long time. Hours. All day. I felt hypnotized by that steady, slow, slow voice in the warm room and by the fingers turning the yellow pencil. I began to yawn and repeat myself endlessly. Then suddenly he laid the pencil down. He began to wrap things up. His hands began to move quickly, to stack his notes and papers. His assistants were very silent, keeping their faces down the way people do when something dangerous is swelling about them. A strange feeling fell over the room.

I began to realize how the police hated us in this town. It was like a hard wall of water, this hatred, that lapped and pushed against us, pressing us backwards, menacingly towards some safety line where they might still continue pushing, trying to show us. In a certain rage my attorney was shouting, *You have no right...no right to keep on like this. She doesn't even have to talk with you, you know that! We're here out of courtesy. Out of respect for the network of laws...the formalities on which this world goes 'round. And I advise you to show some of the same respect.*

Now the detective loses it, turns all his anger on me, his face boiling red because he hasn't got the best of me. Hasn't made me cry. I know now I will never have to cry. My courage is up and nothing will pull it back down. I don't' care how rapt his hate is. *And you, you, lady! I want you to know nobody around here is fooled by your queenly act!* He shouts at me, points his finger almost in my face. My lawyer tries to step in, tries to get between us, but the detective moves to the side and continues speaking loudly, although beginning to calm himself. *I'll say this. Here's the way I see it. Off the record. Here is what I see.* My attorney relaxes, his face sharpens with curiosity; this could be helpful to him later.

Everyone looks ruffled and troubled. I don't think the detective has behaved like this before. He looks shaken with a queer contempt and malice. *You, lady! I tell you that you wrote that ransom note yourself!* He is breathing with difficulty now.

It sticks out all over once I have talked with you. I can hear your voice in that note the whole way. But what I haven't understood, what we didn't, couldn't figure out is this: if you wrote the note to cover up the murder for any reason whatsoever, how could you? How could a woman sit down and write a ransom note two pages long, knowing her child has just been killed and is lying dead just below her in the basement of the house?

That's because she doesn't know, my lawyer says in a confused outburst.

Exactly. She doesn't know, the detective answers. She doesn't know because she believes the child is not dead. She believes the child is somewhere else. She believes the child is with a man she trusts completely. A man who has been in her house all evening. She knows he was in the house because she put him there. You put him there didn't you? You probably had him in the child's room. In the closet or under the bed. Or even walking around among the guests with a drink in his hand. Maybe in the basement. Maybe you went down in the basement to check on him from time to time. Who would know? Maybe he was down there with the notepad, and each time you bounced in, you composed a few more lines, with him whispering to you. Maybe you had to have what you had to have right then and there! Who would know?

So, you knew he was going to take her out of there. You thought there would be a big news day, right? That was the plan you're talking about in your notes. You expected him to take her and then call your home in the ruse of asking for ransom. Right?

You waited. You waited. You watched the time. But that phone call never came, did it? It must have been maddening. Did it ever dawn on you what kind of dangerous mind you were dealing with? Did you have to wait until they carried your dead daughter up the stairs before you realized what you had been playing with?

You couldn't believe it, could you? Why, he had been so obedient, so eager to please and follow your wishes. How could he betray you this way? How could he put his hands on your daughter like this?

Leave my client alone, let her be now, Michael. You've had your little say, my attorney tells him. He lets me lean against his shoulder since my husband has left the room. He lets me lean against him although I am not shaken by all this drivel. Who would believe such crazy nonsense?

These are the minds that are supposed to be looking for the criminals among us! Supposed to be protecting us!

My attorney tells me it doesn't matter what Mike says. He had to showboat for the department. Believe me, the cops love it when something like this happens to people like us. It proves something to them. But we're not talking to them again. We are finished with the police. We're going teach the American people a little civics lesson with this case. They don't know their own laws. Americans don't. They only know what the cops tell them on TV shows!

After I came home from seeing the police, our friends gathered at our home. Our minister came and we had a prayer service. We all knelt on the floor, holding hands in a circle. I knelt with my swollen, tear-stained face while the prayers rose around me. Someone started a song. They sang "Precious Jesus Take My Hand." My heart was flooded with hope then and I seemed to settle.

My sister arrived from out of town and we had to go to the airport to pick her up. The hours went on and on. The days passed. No leads turned up. Sometimes I put my head in my hands and weep because of the stupidity of this world, the stupidity of forces that are supposed to protect this city. How can any of us be safe when the police are only interested in showing off, making up lurid stories? Why don't they look for the killer? Why are they looking at me? Haven't I been looked at enough in my lifetime? What do they want to see in me? Want to tear me apart and put me on little glass slides to be studied under a microscope, twenty-five billion slides to examine?

I can feel the frustration in people. People all the time calling us, yelling at us on the street, taunting and threatening me. They turn most of their spite on me. Because they see in me a woman who has had everything they want and they can't take it away from me. They will not get anything away from me. They will have to bear that, for I am keeping on, I'm going ahead.

I take courage in the fact that summer will soon be over and drive the spies from their places staked out on the bluffs and beaches. The rains will begin in a few weeks. The leaves will fall and swirl away. They always do. The sky will grow a deeper, deeper blue. Even that young girl with her boyfriend, the two of them still carrying around that battered guitar, hiding by the mailbox waiting for me to appear, to give them a little story. They will have to go. Jumped out right in front of my car last night, yelling to me with the wind carrying their frizzy hair back like two grass mats. *Hey, Patsy! Mrs. Ramsey! People are waiting to hear from you! You know that! Hey, Patsy! Mrs. Ramsey! People are roused to screaming. Roused to intimacy with you over what has happened. They want to wallow in your secrets. Want you for their talk shows. Those vivid, soul-burning secrets. America wants someone to pour your secrets into their ears. Why not let us do that for them, Patsy? Patsy, the ears of America are burning up to hear a whisper from you!*

Well, let 'em burn, I laugh. Let 'em burn until no one in America has any ears left on the sides of their heads, just little wadded-up, melted-down globs.

That's how you know an American anywhere. How you pick one out. By his smoking ears. Ears smoking on the side of his head.

I think this is funny. I call this over my shoulder as I quickly rush away, laughing. And in a few steps I reach my front door. I grab the metal knob in my hand and turn it. It is locked, of course. Double-locked. I like the feel of its solid resistance to pressure. A pressure that easily gives way to my key, and in a second I am inside, out of range of the yelling voices.

I stand alone, catching my breath. I do not turn on the light. I just stand there, alone in this dark. Where I know so much.

Nothing but Idolatry

IF THERE IS IDOLATRY ANYWHERE IN THESE UNITED STATES, IT'S got to be in the trailer worshipers around my part of Appalachia. I mean, these people will bow right down to the ground in front of any old trailer — and the older and more beat up these trailers are, the longer they've been abandoned and boarded shut, the more eagerly they're worshiped.

That's why I can move any old trailer in here into the farthest reaches of these backwoods, down the most isolated, pothole-ruined dirt road you can think of, where no living soul has traveled for months, and in no time at all the mecca begins. Blinky-faced people come rattling up in dust-covered cars, slow and seeking in manner, drawn as if some hereditary social instinct has kicked in. They put on their brakes and come to a full stop and sit there, looking at this rusting hump of a thing, lying like an animal just hauled in before taking its last, collapsing breath in the tall weedy marsh groves.

Then everyone wants it. They knock on your door. They want to rent it. Want to fix it up. Give you anything you want. They'll know its history, backwards and forwards, like reciting the plagues in the Bible.

"That's the one Louis and Sue used to own, ain't it?" they'll tell you. "I'd recognize that trailer anywhere. I've seen me some big times in that front room. They held card games in the kitchen. Remember everything now. See these holes right here over the door? Them holes went in there the night Earl Watts got shot right in the yard. He had been winning big all evening off of Tude Stamper; I remember like it was last night. But then he got up and went outside like he might walk off without giving Tude a chance to win something back. Stood under that big blue bug light Sue kept. Can still see it snapping and sizzling bugs like shooting stars in the dark.

"Well, I saw Tude was real quiet. Too quiet. Tude never could take losing. Saw him reach in his pocket and take out a ball of candy and put it in his jaw, and then reach in again. I seen him push someone off of a porch once for making fun of his pup, what a ugly little thing it was. Pushed him hard, too.

"Then I saw him reach in again, take out the gun. 'Son,' I said, 'I'm begging to you, don't do that. I'm begging to you.' He kept on moving that ball of candy 'round in his mouth, then he done it. He's got cancer now. Can't shit. Can't piss. People ask me how he is, and I tell 'em, 'you figure out how he is if he can't shit and can't piss.'

"Of course we came right back the next fall. Hunting deer. Full gang of us boys. Built big fires on the creek bank. Hung those deer up in the trees. Give the guts to the dogs and cats. The women stayed in the kitchen over the frying pans. They had the beer out, too. And this old Doodle Gates, he liked television better than any man I'd allow there ever was...one night he's in there watching television in the front room. So drunk, he didn't know what in hell he was watching. It was that movie *The Fly*, the one from the '50s. It buzzed on and on with him watching.

"And I was looking at him from another room, suddenly seeing his eyes getting round like he's a man five stories up, looking down with no alternatives to jumping out of a window. He gets up and comes running... 'I tell you what,' he said, 'That son of a bitch in there is hungry!' Running and stumbling his whole body against the door frame. And out he takes and goes running into everything in his way.

"Somebody else lived there, too, once. That Sissy Jones and Lloyd. Couldn't have no kids. The doctors sent them all over, trying to find out if Lloyd was shooting blanks or if Sissy needed another hole punched in her somewhere. Cost the government plenty. And finally she got herself pregnant. Had the baby. But don't you know she didn't have that baby but ten days when she gave it away for adoption. Said she didn't want it. Wanted another kind. Wanted a good baby. They put her ass in the asylum..."

Now, they used to break the trains off in compartments beside the rails and people lived in them. Then when they made highways, that's when they got these trailers, which are like a form of rail car. And we crawl back to them like back to the womb.

My daddy loved the rails. Wherever the rails took him, wherever there was work, hauling him back and forth to make some money. Down to the furniture factories in North Carolina. Those bean-canning factories. Sawmills. So I guess a trailer looks like the last car on one of these trains. Turned over in the meadow of time.

"I'll fix it up if you want to rent it to me," they say. "Put in some windows. Tar the roof. Hunting rights come with it?"

Each time you rent it and someone moves out, it goes downhill a little bit more. It's always the same. They are crazy eager to move in. You've never heard such stories they tell to get in. Then once they're in there, it's never like they thought it would be. They start to fall behind in the rent. Let the garbage pile up. And one day you find they've abandoned it. Stiffed you. But just when you're getting ready to send the sheriff after them, here comes one of their buddies wanting the place. Ready to lay down his money in cash. They all know each other from down at the employment office.

I was going to burn the goddamnn thing down, set it on fire and be rid of it. I already had the match in my hand when I heard the truck slow down and a man's voice calling to me, "You own that trailer?"

"What's left of it, I do." I don't even turn my head until I'm finished pouring on the kerosene.

"The Hugharts said so. Said you owned it." The Hugharts had just moved out. I put my match down. He's a man about 60, I'd allow, facing him close up in the sun.

"You know me?" he asked, with something a little mournful in his voice, like I'm supposed to know.

"Am I supposed to know?"

"No, but I just thought I'd ask. My name is Collinsworth."

"Well, yeah, I know of the Collinsworths. Biggest and oldest family in the county, if not the happiest. The most common, you'd say. Lot of them lived here at one time, I bet. Lived in this trailer, huh?"

"My daddy lived in it. But you didn't know about it. The trailer sat down in Shoulderblade then. Next to the river. Flood carried it 40 miles back into Black Snake. Lodged it on the sandbar where my daddy and some of them boys hauled it all the way back to Hazard. It's been around. Yes, sir. You didn't know my daddy, did you?"

He can forget his little ol' daddy stories. I've heard them, ever last one. He's not getting in here.

"I knew your own daddy a long time ago," he said. "When the trains still ran through here."

I look at him. Getting close to each other is part of making your living down here; I understand that well enough.

"Your daddy was in a World War II prison camp, wasn't he?" he asked, looking back over his shoulder at the trailer stuffed with bags of rubbish. "Japs got him."

"We got them back though, didn't we? What about it?"

"Well, I'll tell you something," he answers. "I was just a little tyke back then. Real hot dusty day in spring. April 6, 1947. Hanging around the post office that day."

"What day was that?"

"Why, the day your father came back from the war on the train, don't you know? I was just there, hanging around, watching the men whittle and talk. The war had been over a long time then," he went on in the same breath all of them have; intense, fluvial, never-ending. "Two years. Yes, sir. But everybody who was going to come back had already come back. Or so we thought. Even most of the dead had been set down off the trains in coffins. But your dad was still missing. We had given him up."

I stared at him, and fingered the matches. "Your mother was working up at the Mission Building. She was his sweetheart before he left. She never looked at another man after she heard he was missing in action. I guess they told you about it."

"Tell you the truth, it's a subject we never liked. Never mentioned."

I said, "So you don't know what I'm telling you?"

I shook my head.

"Well, it was bright and hot that morning when the train come in. It sat there on the tracks in the sun. We saw something was unusual. For the conductors to get off and just stand there, like they were waiting on somebody."

"'What is it, boys?' one of the fellows on the porch asked, standing up. Then a man, looked like a stick man, got off the very last car of the train and walked out with short steps, like he could hardly move in his clean-pressed uniform. He had on his soldier's cap, too. He'd been in a hospital, you felt. The train conductors took off their caps as he came forward. You should have seen the happy look on his face. We were all watching him when all of a sudden a woman recognized him, fell to her knees in the dust with her hands raised over her head, screaming.

"'Look at that, boys,' one of the men said, 'It's Gerald Noble Gerald Noble...He's come home.' And they all got up and went to him.

"I was just a little guy then, like I said, but somebody grabbed me and told me to run up the road to the mission and ask for Minnie Lou and tell her. So I run. Say, you got a cigarette?"

"Got one someplace. Well, did you find her? What did she do?"

"Oh, I had no trouble a tall. I was out of breath a little. I fell on the steps and started yelling, 'Minnie Lou, Minnie Lou. I need to see Minnie Lou.' Oh, I put on a show, all right. And when she got there she looked at me, frightened, and said before I could even open my mouth, 'The train's come in with Gerald on it, hasn't it? Hasn't it?!'

"I nodded to her and she grabbed me. She was shaking all over. She was young and good-looking as they come. You had a pretty mommy. You got a cigarette?"

"Well, did she follow you back to the station?"

"No, I'll say she didn't. She just went in and started fixing herself. Her face was going to look fat next to his no matter what she did to it. We could hear her praying. All the mission women fell to praying, too. See, nobody knew he was alive until the day he stepped down. You going to use that match?"

He stood a minute, studying, then said, "Say, if you're going to burn that trailer up..."

I thought his next words would be to let him live in it a few months first, but he said only, "I'd like to tell a few people about it 'fore you do. I think they might want to watch."

"Go get them," I said. "I can wait."

He disappeared, driving over the little bridge. You can't believe half of what people say. I thought I'd never see him again. But sure enough, just before dark, here they all came in a line, rattling up the road in the same old cars with the same old tailpipes dragging on the ground. From somewhere the dogs appeared. And some people walking with a lantern. One woman was carrying a naked baby. When I struck the match, the whole gang of them started. Low at first, then a full, deep-from-the-bone hollering.

I swear to God, it's nothing but idolatry. They're all in on it. Every last one of them.

The Whole World is Watching You

IN OCTOBER, WITH FALLEN LEAVES THREE FEET DEEP OVER THE town, Wiladean turned ninety. We gave her a nice birthday party with a flaming cake, expecting beyond expectation that perhaps this time she would finally say something pleasant to us, for she owned such a fortune. But alas, it was not to be. Once we were all seated and silent with our eyes on our little bird-like auntie, balanced in a large chair under her feathered hat, she said in a matter-of-fact voice that none of our lives meant anything. Not a thing. And that old age (if we really wanted to know) was something like eating shit with a splinter. Nobody knew us; we were so common that if the whole family had never been born, what difference would it have made?

"It's not supposed to make any difference. Not that I can see," Bonnie Jean said, very carefully taking to her lips a spoonful of ice cream as if it were on a splinter. "Being famous, if that's what you mean, Auntie, is a very abnormal condition. I'm just glad I'm normal, that's all."

"Normal?" the old dear said with her lipstick-red mouth turned down in a scoff. That's the way she is, negative, negative. Everything negative. Being old has nothing to do with it. She's always been that way, just snotty to the last breath. She goes down here to this Methodist church where she keeps them all mad and fighting each other half the time. Spreading stories about us to them. That our family burned books during the anti-German wave in 1914. Or that an uncle who was crazy killed his dachshunds because they were German. As if it all happened just last week, too, and no one should speak to us. It's things like that! But what can you do?

Goes right on talking as if people didn't come and tell us every word that falls out of her mouth. Not that she has to go anywhere to talk. She talks right now, openly, like we're not even in the same room listening! About me, for example. Joanne. Her dead sister's only daughter: *That Joanne. Sandy's daughter.* I tell you last week when she walked into that church with her hair pulled back from her face like that, I've never been so ashamed of another human being in my whole life. How can she just let herself go like that? You'd think she would know by now what being ugly will do for a woman. The whole world is watching us all. Even Bonnie knows that. Joanne getting up there, too. Forty-something. And she'll never make it in real estate with that hair and those big, ugly capped teeth. And those little painted-on eyebrows. I know she's been to college, but when you add up her other problems she'll have to go further than college to get herself a man.

So, that's me. Now you know all about me. The one who will never make it, who'll never get a man and I sure as hell don't grieve over it. Although she's got me trapped worse than any man might. Sticking her big bank account under my nose as if I'm ready to take off with it in my mouth like a rat with a MasterCard. So I take care of her. She never married, either. But, oh, you should hear her talk about the men who wanted her! That's what I'm here for, to listen to that.

We've lived together since my mother's death, in her old house with the long drafty hallways laid with worn oriental rugs and rife with that Evening in Paris perfume she has kept since World War II. Cobalt blue bottle. She must have a little put on her clothes each evening, after I do her hair, part it in the middle, then do the braids and wrap them around her head.

We have dinner at seven, right after the news, which always disgusts her, and has her sneering right through dessert and tea. After the meal and dishes we go in to the computer. That's when it all changes, that's when science does what God couldn't, for it's the only time any happiness descends. I knew she would love the computer, and it's her money that bought it, but I dare not mention such a thing. I knew Wiladean must think of everything herself. She must never be told what she wants or needs. That's for her to say. So one day I began to feel her shadow falling across the screen as I sat there on the chats.

"It's just typing." she said. "If you can learn it, I can learn it."

I showed her a few things since she asked. How to begin, how to turn it off, and she was quick, really; her mind has not changed much in twenty years. I knew she had been a whiz at typing. "I won the prize in speed," she reminded me. "Boy, that burned certain jealous-hearted people to a crisp." She laughed, showing her small, natural teeth, which she cares for really well, brushing and polishing like priceless china. "But now my fingers are stiff."

"Soak 'em." I said. "Go in there to the sink and soak 'em in hot water. Then we'll cut the tips out of a pair of gloves. Put them on and that will keep them warm and limber."

So each morning now she soaks her hands before she begins, confident and arrogant as a surgeon getting ready to cut something open. Once she discovered the chats she was fascinated to the bone and couldn't get enough.

And the message boards, on which a person can say exactly what one wants when one wants to say it, is a great thing for someone like Wiladean who can't hold back a thought. So great that even a little light of gratitude has crept into her eyes...as if...as if brilliant people knew exactly what she needed and invented it. Gave her the magic she had always been seeking. Pure magic. Neither of us had much respect for science before. Those builders of neutron bombs, atom smashers and the like. Not until the computer did we see what science could do for the human race. It silenced it. Never did we realize how irritating the human voice is. Ideas are great. It's the sound of them we hated, we decided.

Now we are talking about a national hats-off day to these scientists. Never an idle moment for her now. The Gun Control Lounge is one of her favorites. There she uses her masculine screen name, BilliJack44. Who knows what they say to each other in there. Anyway, I am free to go as I please once again with her occupied this way. I go to lectures up at the university, just three blocks away.

There in the old theater I watch all the old-movie classics alone. The old Bette Davis and Joan Crawford films. Johnny Belinda. Jane Eyre while Wiladean plays on the computer until she grows tired. The doctor has ordered special glasses, blue-blockers, for her to wear since she's on there so much, and she wears them, like a creature from the depths of space. But hark! Last Wednesday I'm sitting in there, in the steep rows of seats of this little dingy theater, when I see someone I know — my heart takes a leap — Professor Roar of the English department.

English composition and poetry are his thing. His photograph was in the paper when he received a grant to build a website for his e-zine, *Mud Hill.* Nice romantic name. *Mud Hill.* Probably stole it from someone. A long, snooty face, carefully climbing among the crowd, nodding to no one. Arrogant but somehow handsome, waspy, melancholy, perhaps Hungarian, who can say? But still vaguely repelling. Still cruel. How would he know that just an hour ago we, Wiladean and I, logged into his life? Right there in our living room we stared at his ugly, sensual, snooty face and studied him up close: Dr. Roar received his advanced degrees in neo-expressionism and led the movement in the arch-conservative American Midwest, a challenge still in its development. Cambridge, Oxford, Harvard.

There he sits, his long naked neck just two seats in front of my eyes. Picks his nose nonchalantly, rolls something around in his fingers, cunningly rests his arm over the back of the seat, as if no one can see into the illumination that ramifies out from his important center. It would blind any small eye he imagines to watch him, digging into the center of life, the great knot of truth at the end of his finger.

We sent him in some poems for his *Mud Hill*. Sent him a dozen or more. Only to be told "*Please! Read the Submission!*" He always responds in the same testy way. After a few days comes a reply to the submission: "I have read your poem with careful consideration and I will not keep it."

He was joined in the old theater by three young men, who were late. Came leaping up the steps, carrying raincoats over their arms and talking wildly. Upper-class look about them, the skin and hair and sweaters are upper-class. They kept talking over each other, trying to get at Dr. Roar, who apparently holds their destiny in contemptuous consideration. After the movie, one of them stood in the aisle and did an imitation of Bette Davis from the movie, Bette smoking, Betty dragging her fur on the floor: *I don't care! I don't care! Why in hell shooouuuuld I care? Puff,*

puff, puff. When I got home I did the same impression for Wiladean. Because it was stuck in my mind.

"I never liked Bette Davis," she said. "She's got eyes like a decapitated fish, if you ask me." Ol' negative Wiladean!

Nothing to do then all day. That was last Sunday afternoon. "Why not," she said, "send in some more poems to *Mud Hill*?" Wiladean typed one in. "How about this one: "If You Are Bitten by a Snake," by Wiladean Hargis. Or "Three Signs of Frost Bite"?" Decided on the snake poem.

(*If you are bitten by a snake, turn off your radio. Don't listen to another word from anyone. Leave by the backstairs. Remember the snake probably started out same as you, bored half out of his mind in the Garden of Eden with no one to talk with except those two people walking around without their genital cover on. Think how the snake thinks. The most beautiful creature ever imagined. Think of Eve in its powers, under the great anaconda night, under the stars, the winds of Eden soft, soft in the moonlight then, sharp and wild where the deep fangs went in.*)

"Why, Auntie, I love it! It's great. I bet he will take it. I just have a feeling he will be impressed. It's so unusual." I gave her a hug and kiss. I love poetry.

"*You have mail!*" rang out the automated voice. *MudHill@aol.com*. "I have read your poem, 'If You Are Bitten by a Snake,' very carefully and I am not going to keep it."

So it was over so suddenly. She replied to the message, rather white in the face, "That's O.K. The poem has just been accepted elsewhere, so don't worry." We thought that would be it, since Roar was so laconic and dismissive but to our surprise the voice again announced, "*You have mail!*" We knew it must be Roar because no one else writes us. We were half afraid to log it up and sat there staring at the screen, hugging each other.

"*Oh, that's wonderful!*" began the message. "*You didn't tell me your snake poem was being looked out by other editors. I supposed I have saved half the editors in the continental United States a great disappointment.*"

Her fingers did not hesitate now; they went flying like little fairy fingers over the keyboard. "*Really, I don't understand your last remark. It is a little confusing. What does 'looked out by editors' mean? Maybe you are overcome with anger. But to make multiple submissions is a common practice among the better publications.*"

Now he wrote back. "*I'll have you understand I am well enough aware of the 'better magazines,' thank you. I have published in the most respected journals here and in Europe for the past twenty-five years. I have in fact just come back from a big committee meeting with some of the most highly regarded editors in the world. WE know that the world is watching us. One of our longest discussions was on policy, dealing with careless submissions that tend to overwhelm electronic publications, and what to do about them. I suggest you read my report.*"

There followed an enormous amount of written material. It meant nothing to us. But we were laughing harder than we had done in years. I had to brush away the tears, especially when Wiladean wrote something she had heard on one of the chats: "Oh, wow, Professor Roar sounds hot enough to fuck."

"Auntie, oh, my God!' I screamed. Unfortunately, Roar wanted to continue the fight. Several pages now followed in which he wrote Wiladean's name in capitals as if she should be ashamed of it.

"I just don't think you cut it, Roar," she wrote him back. "Sounds like you woke up this morning with the cocksucker blues."

"Auntie, my God Almighty!"

"*And if you send any more letters like this to me,*" she continued, "*I'm coming over there, DR. ROAR, and dragging your ass out in the road.*"

No reply.

That was the end of their correspondence. For three days she was delighted but then the euphoria started to wear off. I know she hopes he'll write back tonight. What better piece of cake than Dr. Roar. I think I can see her mouth watering, her fingers practicing. And if he does, I'm going to jump in on the fight with both hands myself. Going to tell him if wants to pick that big nose of his in this town, like he did in the theater the other night, he better think where he rolls his boogers and throws them. Because the whole world is watching.

Things That Make People Unclean

THE PRISON WHERE THE ISRAELIS KEEP US LIES QUIET AS A STONE upon the low sandy formation of a ridge. A dense shimmering curtain of heat is always waving from the fields beyond. Even in spring the land has a fallow, scrub-desert look to it, but at times is actually swampy and full of hard sprouting willows, and right up next to the prison grounds themselves this marshy area is fixed, embedded with deep razor wire; a no-man's land between two high-strung, double coiling metal fences.

On mornings when the fog is low and thick, the Jews in the towers have to depend on dogs to sound a warning if someone comes near these coiling razor enclosures. From the start the prisoners have said these dogs are an added humiliation to their captivity — a forced contact with filth, an unclean thing. But most of this out-crying is just hype to keep the trouble stirred up, and as soon as we see the dogs being led out in the mornings, straining at their leashes to begin the round, I jump with the others to join in on the angry, ceremonial shouting, and a fiercer, wilder timbre shakes in my voice: a desperate reaction due less to any orthodoxy on my own part than to another tension which has been steadily mounting, day upon day as they truck in more Palestinians. Every day these news loads of prisoners seem younger, harsher, more confident, just as crowds around college hangouts get suddenly younger, or arrogant and distant if you stay in school too long.

That I've found myself too long in both places is obvious. Three years here in the one of the hardest camps the state of Israel has going for "terrorists," and before that I was in the university.

Never mind which university that was...but if you've kept up with the news only casually, you already know the place. And it won't surprise you when I say it took me eleven years to finally get that law degree. Because of the turmoil and the disruptions. The Jewish militia was always running in on one wild rumor after another and getting the people they wanted. Arresting faculty right off the podiums and rounding up entire classrooms which they trucked away to detention centers where no family or friend could find them for months. So you've got to be deaf or living in some little far-away prison of your own making perhaps, not to have heard mention of what I'm talking about.

If what I am talking about does not seem dreadful enough, let me tell you what it feels like, for they are two different things entirely. What I am talking about will eventually get into the history books, but what it feels like will be forgotten. Here is what it feels like: You are a man facing a world that suddenly does not believe in right and wrong, but believes what is good for himself is right, but what is good for you is wrong. You cannot make him see it any other way, and just trying to explain this causes him to laugh in your face. Eventually, if you persist with your philosophy and complaining, you get something more in your face. I have had all sorts of things in my face, let me tell you. Angry shouts, exposed teeth, spit, fists, guns with triggers clicking, stupid mouths twisting like the death throes of a snake. You get used to some of it. You expect the hate, for after all, this is an infuriating war, especially to the Americans who pretend they are supporting nothing but a sixty-year-old street fight and go on waiting for us to lie down before their little technological monster they have planted among us. We will not do that.

So you come to expect the terror. You prepare, build yourself up like a tough callous of a thing, but deep inside the callous is a softness that quickens each time you remember certain things. When I was free, I still was not safe. I didn't know what being safe meant. After I was sixteen I knew I and the others were being watched by a hostile authority. And each time I was fingered and brought in and locked up and questioned, the anger went deeper and more bitterly into me than before, until it was like I don't know what, like barbed wire, like one single string of the stuff was being pulled back and forth across your naked skull cap, indifferently, by a bored hand. Just to take your time. Your life. Just to keep you from living. We used to laugh together, my gang of friends and I, at the primitive drive behind the ambition of our oppressors. They do not want us to live, not around them, and not anywhere. This is the lesson you take into your everyday mind. And if you have a soul, it gets into it as well and turns it ugly and sour, like one of those old houses shot to hell but left standing for some unknown reason in the border area, so you cannot hide the mad distortions and flashes of hatred you feel inside from anyone. Then if you are here, in foul captivity, nothing reminds you of freedom so much as the sight of a gun. One of those lightweight revolvers made in America or Italy, gleaming like a black smile on the uniformed hip of a guard. How I dream of placing my hands on one of them! Feeling it under the curl of my fingers, cold and serious and friendly as an angel.

I'm always dreaming; you see that now. I carry dreams that fairly break me down, until I forget that it's been days since I really talked with anyone, for example. You get into moods.

You find yourself sitting among the other prisoners at times, squinting, your eyes lowered, your fingers pinching a cigarette and your foot upon the squirming neck of all memory. You sit there and you ride around in your mind, knowing there is nothing to give you ease at times like these, nothing to lift you off the black hook of this creaking overloaded carousel the enemy has hung you on for all these months. For years. For the rest of your life, perhaps.

You keep yourself a little stiff and numb with trying. You don't want to remember certain faces. How they lifted and pressed warmly against your own, for it could start you yearning so fiercely you would kill someone for just bumping into you. And the music. The radios, although hard to come by, are a great torture at times. Just a scrap of music, a flinging ditty twittering in upon the burning air from a lone transistor is enough to send the past dancing through your heart. You remember exactly where you were then years ago as some old jazz piece cries to you, so caressingly, so beseechingly intimate, the sounds seem made out of the willing flesh itself, and to be drifting in the nerves like booby traps in a flowing ditch, silently, sorrowing, waiting to hit the air and burst alive. But you keep it down and save it. You let it wait. For your waiting fits into things here, another lurking influence camouflaged against the hard, baked centuries of this place.

What do I look like? That's the first thing any mind jumps to. The head with its strong black hair, the eager eyes and brow...you probably already have me well imagined. This person who just came up from out of nowhere, so to speak, and started telling you his problems. Dark, of course, a little above average in height, the classical Arab face to which some of the trashy adolescent arrogance still clings. Shoulders a little stooped. Glasses — I wear specs, but not thick ones, held together now with rigging from wire off the fence. The best we could do, and they give me a soft look, a scholarly look, not like who I really am, someone forever ready to die. Day after day, ready for death. It shows in my face, around the eyes when I look in the mirror on shaving day, a sad misty grief for everything, for everyone. Even the Jews.

In the good days when I was free, I lived on the very edge of the university campus, where the new buildings blended into the old city slums. I had a thick-walled, white-washed little room over an old theater. Other students had similar quarters in the building. We shared a kitchen at the end of the hallway, with a battered refrigerator secured with a locked chain draped around its middle like a sword belt on a fat knight. Only Mustafa B., part-time student and baker's assistant, had the key and would open it only once a day, at which times we cooked on a little charcoal fire in the back yard under the wall.

The theater down below was ancient, large, and ornate with battered, carpeted floors and tall, rose and green colored windows like a great room set aside for balls in a once-beautiful but now decaying palace. *The Ten Commandments* ran there for years. Everyone knew it word for word. When it was frayed to tatters, a John Wayne festival replaced it.

Although it was summer and the town was dead, students would come and fill up the place just because it was basically free, and to practice their English by mouthing the new lines along with the cowboys and Indians. It was some of the best fun we'd ever had, chanting like that, mimicking in that strange accent, hollering about the wars way out west in Oklahoma and Cheyenne. Move back and try to see us in the theater seats. The Indians before us bigger than gods, barbaric and howling, painted all over in gorgeous wild colors, flying down the passes on their fast ponies with flaming arrows whizzing...everything glittering on the high, wild screen while we applauded from our dark cave below, cheering on the burning wagon trains, the galloping wonderful Apache, the great Comanche, even as they fell through the air in every direction with their arms and legs outstretched against the great green and brown American prairie.

Weeks later, after the Israeli police came and boarded up the place, I still lived there. I would enter the side door as if nothing had happened, bouncing up the stairs as if the police had cleared all the others out of my way at my special request. Eventually my friends returned as well, one by one. Sometimes we would throw big beer parties and get wild on kat and start hooting the lines out of the John Wayne films. Our voices brought people looking up at the windows. Sometimes low drums thudded in with the shouting. Shouting gives you such confidence. Just the sheer physical assertion of it does something to you. We shouted for horses. We wanted our ponies. And women. More guns and money from Washington. This confidence irked the police, who were back by the end of summer to finish off the nest of rats, as they called us. I was the first to be taken in and jailed. Charged with having an unlicensed phone. And "habitation of a suspected dwelling." Maps and graffiti had been found on the walls along with streets of former bombing sights circled and marked with X's, and drawn on the stairs were obscenities of the police wearing cowboy boots and sucking their thumbs while they ran naked, shooting off their weapons at fleeing students.

There was a special way you had to stand during the interrogation. I couldn't get it right. I kept turning to the officer, a man about my own age, who wanted me to look straight ahead with my hands cuffed behind my back and one leg chained to the table like a dog as he talked non-stop.

"Why were you shouting about burning things? Fires? Ponies? Horses? Guns? Who's running guns into the campus area? Where in hell do you get the idea of ponies into your feeble-minded brains? And why are you bastards always shouting? Why this goddamnn obsession with your own sons-o'-bitching voices? Never mind. Face the wall, please. Explain what you know about his latest bombing, please!" He was holding a little whip in his hand. I was silent.

"And this latest piece of garbage sent to the police a so-called poem sent in to the police headquarters. The police do not read poetry. We are our own art form, or haven't you heard?" He took an envelope out of his pocket. It was very crumbled as if it had been passed around to various sweaty hands for days. "Listen to this. Listen closely." He began to read in a rather experienced voice, beating a kind of time with his whip. I think he must have been in love with poetry at one time. You can tell such people. But he had given it up for this foreign experiment his religion put on him. His assistants watched my face.

"Old Land." That's the title of this great epic we found among your papers. Exactly like the one sent here. "Old Land." O.K. "*To be born in Gaza is to feel yourself even in sleep picked at by an ancient sea and wind, to be spotted in your bed like grey debris, the twisted leg of history, washed up on a beach in front of a crowd, searching your ears with flash-lights for the last dangerous word you might have heard.*" "Oh, tell me one thing: did the author feel he was a real smartass when he wrote this last line? I bet it would make me double over if I could have seen his face!" I stood silent.

He gave me a sneering look and continued. "*While in your cool dreams, under the high galleons of morning, a sailor like yourself filled with risky love of the deep, runs on down some steps, folding on and on beneath his feet like the meals laid down in the stomachs of rich tourists, carried laughing and chatting in taxi cabs, like topaz dolphins might, leading the way through waves of opal joy.*" Here he waited for me to look at him, expecting something more, to prove I knew there was more to the poem. I did not change my expression.

"*Oh, to have your own spot on this earth, to have it pure in character as a theme park. To have all truths fall about you, like the stopped hearts of sun-sucked apricots, dropping between the sugary lips of some wild and nervous mouth, oh to be only among your own kind, though someone calls to you from the dogged shadows of Jerusalem's long and blood throat: Hey, you, Smiley-face, the whole world suffers for you, but bait your rat traps with what you want. We chew my own black crust of hope.*"

"Why did you send this crap to our headquarters? Do you think this world runs on poetry?"

"No. I pay no attention to anything that runs," I said in low voice, so he shouted to me to speak up and raised his whip, trying to make me flinch. He crumbled the poem and tossed it in the wastebasket next to his desk. Then he picked up a newspaper and pointed to a photograph of what was an explosion.

"And this! Explain please what you know about the latest bombing. The bus on Wednesday, on its way to the beach with seventy-five people in it. All ten tires blown in ten directions across town. You think that will do something to our tourist trade? Finish it off or something?

Not a dent! Not a dent. Not one less tourist for us, but one less little filthy bug on the streets around here. There is going to be one less bug creeping around the slums where you live. You understand, of course, what we do with cockroaches?"

I replied in a whisper, my lips barely moving, and pointed to heaven with a shrug. This cryptic gesture unsettled the interrogator. I think I must have been the first Arab he ever struck, for after his hand blazed across my face and I fell backwards to the floor in my handcuffs, something happened to him. His anger drained away in embarrassment. He turned his back, but I could still see he was very red in the face, his neck flushed red, and he threw his whip against the wall, into the corner. It was strange. He looked tired and worn out to the bone. His name was Milton. Milton something. That was years ago.

The appearance of more guard dogs, huge, low-slung German Shepherds that creep stealthily about on their hind toes, is causing a constant buzz of discussion among the religious faithful in the camp. Some of these faithful are just what the Jews suspect them to be: cold, rigid, dangerous fanatics who would probably dismember a hand that has risked polluted contact with a dog.

"I hate 'em dogs!" declares Jabra-Jabra, who has been studying English. "Only the very dirty people in our village, the outcasts, kept them. We could hear them at night barking, but we were not allowed by our families to go near them."

"But why, my teacher, are dogs considered more dirty than other animals?" asks a young man. He already knows the law but is a born lackey, a stepped-on worm who is always begging for a little more attention. The teacher, too, loves to be consulted.

"Because the dog, he parades about with his genitals shining and proud and goes in for public copulation. He is always attending to his genitals, licking and mounting, not caring who is watching."

"It is not good to see one thing upon the back of another, enjoying."

"But the Jews are very advanced. They will make it seem right," says Jamil, who grinds his white teeth with a bitter, serious intensity as he sits on his haunches, his arms dangling.

They all sit in a circle. They discuss many things. On the ground before them is an American magazine with pictures of Hollywood stars. An old magazine. The fanatics are allowed all the old magazines they wish, nothing current. Old magazines where they can look and look and denounce the past. Who cares what they say about what happened months ago? Jamil alone turns the pages. The sun blazes down on the frayed, makeshift tent. A hot wind touches their faces.

"Yes. The Jews will make it seem right. They are full of the twentieth century," Jamil says. "And the dog is the most fitting companion for modern man. Especially perfect for the Americans," Jamil continues. His eyes have a perpetual, half-sleepy irritability as he stares down at the open pages of the magazine. "There in America everyone is dirty. You can see by their magazines. My cousins lived in New Jersey. He studied to be a big expert in glass blowing. Heat and sand is all you need, see. But then he started taking pictures of women and that was the end of him. We never heard from him again; he grew into a millionaire. The women there take it off for anybody. Anybody can become a millionaire taking their pictures. It is a great mystery how they love the dirt there, especially that little teaspoon of dirt called Israel.

"Elizabeth Taylor is for the Jews," Jami says further. He is gazing steadily at a picture of Elizabeth Taylor being discharged from the Betty Ford Clinic. "That's a drug clinic franchise where wealthy women go and get all the drugs they want. They take the drugs to make themselves more dirty. It's all they care about. They can't get enough dirt to do them."

"I hate 'em dogs!" Jabra-Jabra declares again. They sit silently in the hot wind now, their arms down, their eyes on the photograph of Elizabeth Taylor. "She marry many times. Like a man," Jamil whispers in a grimace of disgust.

In my dreams, in my sullen breathless escape runs, I have a dog with me. I am hiding in the desert, in a shallow cave, pressed flat to the earth on my stomach and I can feel my heart kissing the ground a hundred-ninety miles a minute. The soldiers are all around me, shouting and shooting. I press my face against the stones and the smell of the old theater comes back to my nostrils, the dank air of the old carpets and fluttering beam of the old projector on my eyes. But it is not the projector's beam that teases my eyes awake, only the sword-stiff shaft of the ever-moving searchlights crossing the compounds from the towers.

I get up and pace the floor. It must be very early morning. Three o'clock or four with the air full of fog. The dog in my dreams fascinates me. Several months ago I actually made friends with one of the guard dogs. The faithful do not know about it. No one knows. She kept sentinel duty outside the storage area which just happened to be located near a section of fence where I might have to go over when I decide to go.

If a prisoner is caught feeding a dog he is severely punished, locked up in a hole for weeks on end with no questions asked, so I had to watch myself. Besides, prison dogs are rigidly trained to be vigilant and sometimes will fly at the throat of an inmate and attack him for the slightest form of friendliness, even for the wrong kind of eye to eye contact, such as prolonged staring or winking, or making faces. So any attempt at feeding is a very risky business.

I know nothing about dogs, nevertheless upon encountering this one dog — it was a young female — I had a peculiar feeling that her viciousness was not a final and irrevocable trait and that behind her cruel mask was something warm that would mingle with me, the enemy.

I began, then, a battle for her affections. First of all I threw her off by showing no trepidation in my walk as I approached her space, and always swung the door back with a careless force, nudging her a little where she was chained up to a jack in the wall.

She submitted to this indignity. And in her extraordinary quiet manner, it was obvious that she was encouraging me. There are signals you recognize after a while if you live the way I have lived. I saw in her a certain need for danger you see in women: that little pretense of mistrust and tension in her knitted brows, while a flash of understanding ran through the perfectly still eyes, as if there were a brighter brain behind her dog's brain. One day I seriously broke the rule by feeding her. I carried a piece of bread in my pocket and flung it down between her paws. It disappeared in a gulp on her tongue like a greasy, grey shadow. Casually I looked around to see if I was being watched. Then I broke another rule: I reached and patted her sleek, burly shoulder, feeling as I did the wonderful strong bones under my hand with a little shock.

I worked in a detail crew that hauled garbage from the kitchens and mess halls each morning and evening. The guard who oversaw us trusted me always to run ahead of the crew and fasten back the large iron doors for the oncoming garbage dumpster. I was expected then to run back and help hold the trolley as it proceeded down the incline to another truck waiting below the loading zone dock. It was at this door my dog stood her guard duty.

As I fastened the door back in place I always dropped some little goody or another between her paws and then hesitated and glanced away at the landscape for a brief second, looking hungrily into the misty distance. It seemed to me one day that the dog imitated my gaze exactly, looked as I did, away and beyond the barbed wire, out to where freedom was, and then back at me, while keeping her body very still and erect — I swear to heaven, in a sly clandestine manner. I can't claim without doubt that she understood what she was doing, but her actions were the actions of a cautious, discernible thinker, if ever actions distinguish the thinking creatures among us.

For example, never once in the next three weeks did she give me away by showing any spontaneous movement of recognition: never did she so much as lift even the tip of her tail, or affect to have any connection with me at all. The times when I was feeding her every day as I quickly ran out to pin back the door, or taking the liberty of petting her in the evening dark, her only reaction was a slow narrowing of the eyes in a suggestive way that made me feel she knew well enough what I was planning for the two of us.

Then, without warning, she vanished from the compound. I discovered her absence the hard way one night by reaching my hand towards a dark shape where she usually sat in the shadows. But instead of touching her warm, tufted head, I was met with a response so diabolic that even now, just thinking about it seems to make the air rattle with those slobbering fangs of the black monster who nearly tore his own head off on the end of the chain holding him jacked to the concrete wall.

Next day this same dog uncovered his teeth in a snarling recognition of me as I stood with a baffled face, scanning the back area for a sight of the former dog, and I was very frightened to see a guard watching me, as if he knew something. But what could he know? And how could he know it? For days sheer paranoia prevented me from mentioning her, but finally I felt safe enough to make my off-hand inquiry and was told that she had been put down because she had suffered a complete nervous breakdown. A frenetic, disturbed restlessness had worn her out. She couldn't sleep or eat. When she tried to lie down, her teeth clattered in her head and her body wouldn't stop quivering. She was sick of being a dog, guarding and watching the prisoners. If she got to her feet she immediately began circling to lie back down. This torture went on for days. Then they shot her. The kennel keeper said this sometimes happened to dogs in a combat zone, but rarely in a watch camp.

I pace about myself, up and down in the smoky, dark corner of the dormitory, heavy with human odors, and filled with prisoners sleeping on mats and cots. Some are awake, propped up on their elbows, smoking and talking in secretive voices, waiting for the call to prayers and breakfast. Down below, night guards with guns patrol inside the two fences. And outside the fence, an electronics warfare officer walks about with his mysterious equipment. And still there are escapes. When an Arab goes, he goes right under their noses, on his toughened bare feet.

This dank morning, the new dog, the one who replaced my friendly animal, is making the rounds with the guards. He is a huge, black and brown German Shepherd with alert, erect ears, and a lowered back as he follows at the guards' boot heels. I knew everything I wanted to know about him in three minutes. Even that they would have to shoot him to get him off any inmate he might attack.

It is not a second later after I am thinking this that the incredible happens. I see the brute shape leap with his powerful agility streaking in the searchlight, followed instantly by horrible human shrieks rising in the foggy dawn and startling all the sleeping inmates behind me. In a crowd we stand watching the soldiers bending over the canine body stretched on the ground, their revolvers drawn. The guard who has actually done the shooting has a look of utter revulsion on his face for the bleeding hairy form with its last breaths sucking in and out of the death-swallowing ribs. The guards become increasingly nervous. A whirl of alarm sirens wakes the entire camp now and men in dusty rags begin rushing like a tidal wave against the fences as the news comes down that an inmate has had his throat torn open by an attack dog. A furious, belligerent chant begins somehow. "*Dirty! Dirty! Dirty! Ah, Dirty!*" we shout in Arabic. "*Dirty! Dirty!*"

The young guard-soldier wipes his face with the back of his hand and still holds the smoking revolver. His face has a painful, nervous baited look on it now.

And it occurs to me again, as it often has these past few days, that the Jews are uncomfortable with dogs. They have traditionally kept themselves far from dogs, as have the Muslims. They are almost as ignorant of the animals as we. What they know, and even why they know it, is because of the Germans. Just as what I know, I know because of them.

"*Dirty! Dirty!*" we shout, thrashing our arms in outrage like devils along the rim of a pit of hell.

Yet afterwards we are very proud of our conduct, the way we held it all together. We remained standing and shouting until the commander himself came and read off the medical conditions of the wounded inmate. The man will not die. We are assured of that. An hour ago he went into surgery at a capital hospital where he was flown by helicopter. His name is Brutros. Only a special few knew about him, but now everyone is discussing his life. He was born in the occupied territory, in the village of X, near Hebron, and is the father of nine children although he is still under thirty. His body is not large. He is red-haired, black-eyed, and pale as a moth. His presence at the fence where the dog discovered him crouched was the result of much planning. In fact, he had studied that fence until his knowledge of everything that went on around and about it was like some amazing, dreamed-up sociology. Imagine a day-to-day study of a hundred feet of stretched barbed wire! It made him think, sitting there, watching who came and went. He was fond of slogans.

"*The hard way is the only way you learn.*" That was one of his favorites. Or, "*While men fight in the fields, the beasts enter their homes.*" That's a good one. Or, "*We are a desert people, we Arabs. A crowd that knows nothing about swimming. To swim, you must constantly keep in mind how all men stop at the ends of their nose holes. To dwell on such an idea is worse than drowning.*" The Jews got to like him. They referred to him as Chic-Koran, or Koran-Chic, terms they probably picked up from the American way of tagging and slinging things.

But now I know only that in the coming days everyone is going to be talking about the same thing: "How's Brutros?" Or "Brutros is still hanging on, so what do you think?" Or "Brutros is dead; now you're really going to see something hung up to dry on those fences! We'll rip this place to pieces so it can't be put back!" That's the way it always is, isn't it? You look at history and you'll see. You'll see that every time a little change takes place, someone gets brutalized, then eventually up come the great terrors. And when there has been enough terror, the enlightenment appears. Finally, the enlightenment. Isn't that the pattern?

And sometimes the start of the enlightenment is so brief it passes unnoticed, no more than a wisecrack or a joke shouted up out of the noisy flow of time. Like this morning, out of the lightened dark of the compound, through the rising placid blue wisps of smoke, someone shouts to the Jews in the towers: "*Give up your religion, I beg you! Drop all this crap that's killing everybody!*"

"*You first!*" they yell back, laughing.

But something else will just take its place. If it isn't one thing, it's another just as bad. So why bother? As Brutros used to say, "If there's a crack, dirt will find it. Especially a crack in the head."

So it passes like that, a little laugh on the wind. And it feels strange, hearing the enemies instruct each other, each telling the other how to pull himself out of the age-old sickness, leaning forward, acting and clowning like fools. Like peeping around a mirror, feeling the imponderable agent of light, glittering and teasing, but utterly hard and sure, so if you face it, no matter what you are, it falls upon you and makes you known.

Our Bodies

AT FIRST THERE WERE FOUR OF US IN THIS ROOM AT THE prison infirmary at X. But two have died. Their bodies are stretched out on the floor without a cover and we must use our hands or take off our shirts to swing at the flies and keep them off the best we can. For this so-called infirmary is simply a bare cell with a table and sink and a ditch of running water, or open sluice...a splashing sewer that enters one side of the room and exits under the wall on the other side, flowing past a complex of other cells in the prison. Several times a day water gushes down the sluice in force then dries to a trickle.

Fawaz, my cell mate and said "terrorist," who refused to be paralyzed by the nauseating stench and normal heat of the place, now faces with me the added torture of two dead bodies the guards will not remove. He begins to examine the remains of a "medicine cabinet," an upright stack of various dirty-looking shelves with cans and empty boxes in the corner. On the bottom shelf stands a fifty-pound metal can that, when the lid is pried open, turns out to contain coarse salt, and its twin metal companion stacked next to it, almost rusted through, is full of finely ground white powder. I thought at first glance it was flour or baking powder perhaps, but Fawaz narrows his eyes and immediately says it is plaster of Paris. "You know what plaster of Paris is used for, don't you? Making casts around broken bones! You see about you the scattered tools of a torture chamber of which broken bones are very common!"

He continues to run his hands through the powder, mumbling to himself in a profane way, looking around for other receptacles which, when he realizes are unavailable, begins to dip up water with a leaky can from the open trench and pour into the salt. Within minutes he has mixed a thick paste that he drags with my assistance the length of the cell to the dead bodies.

Fawaz begins to strip the bodies according to his upbringing, something I am much too squeamish and sick to my stomach to help him with. But he, well tutored in the hygienic believes of the Muslim faith, lays a covering of wet salt over the bodies as a protection to us, an act that spurs his imagination into suggesting we move further along and make coffins of plaster around our dead and have a proper burial for them if I could only swallow my gorge long enough to do as he directed and follow him in the prayers.

"But of course they will come for the bodies shortly," I protest.

"They'll come when the maggots have had their fill, and bones can be tossed in a bag!" he answers in an almost trance of hatred, running and kicking the wall near him, so I understood then that he must be allowed his wish, must be allowed the mechanical activity of preparing the bodies, and the ritual activity of the prayers or he will die as well, and so I join in the Muslim rite, sitting on the floor and beating my breast as the prayer requires for the two brothers who had just completed their lives' last adventure, their souls freed, dropped like fruit from the tree of life, a hard, bitter eternal tree, its roots sunk in the blood baths of a desert orchard, watered on hate and contention, where men fought for every little inch of dirt and air... have now peacefully fallen into a kingdom of love among their brothers — while Fawaz and Ashi, who find themselves alone in hell, are still compelled to do an earthly funeral of farewell. "For not even in death should we suffer the trespassing foot of the enemy," says Fawaz. "Death must be protected from the dishonor of hate. Death, with its black and hooded head, stands above man's hateful greed and greedy wars. Death alone cleanses the infidel and believer alike with a nameless silence.

"Help us, our one God," he now prays in a desperate chanting as we pick up the table at each end and carry it with one dead body, then the other, near the ditch. There Fady, as I now call him, begins mixing the white powder and plastering the clean soft handfuls over the faces of the dead men, thick and smooth. "Good-bye, Mustafa...you did your share," he says, closing the face with a gauze of plaster. "Never did I see fear in this strong face of yours." He pats the mixture over the shoulders and arms and chests, down over the long pale torsos, letting his hands drift soothingly until the bodies gleam half-luminous, like sacred objects in the darkish cell, lifting a freakish glow against the stone walls. "Help us, our one God," Fady prays as he finishes and washes his hands in the sewer.

A single guard comes and looks in the room. He opens his wide eyes towards the back of the cell. "Hey, what's that shit? What the fuck is that?" he asks. "Mummies? Some sort of goddamnn insect get in here and build a nest or something? Ha ha ha. I was told there were dead bodies in here, now where the fuck are they? You mean that's them? A couple of statues? Statues! Ha ha ha!"

Neither Fady nor I speak. From his accent and manner I know the guard is the one who shot off the gas canisters into the cell that killed our friends two days ago. An American. One of those psychos from New York City, and crude as they come. He stares straight into my face, waiting for me to see the letter. In his breast pocket sticks the corner-end of an envelope with neat handwriting on it. My eyes fall on it with greedy excitement, then quickly away as I catch myself. Not smart to show want.

"Yes, it is a letter for you!" the guard laughs with scoffing delight. "And from a woman, too. What's she look like, Ashi? Like a camel, ha ha ha! What else but a camel!" His mouth and eyes seem to sprawl and widen over his face in a flush of arousal out of the deep corruption of cruelty and brutality that lies in him. "What else would you hump but some big, high-ass camel? Ha ha ha ha!"

Still no words from us. We sit on.

He has a clipboard in his hand and is making notes. "Two dead bodies," he hoots as he writes, "And two more than dead. Ha ha ha!"

"You will be sending someone to take the dead bodies out of here, won't you?"

"Shut up! You do not question me about my intentions! Understand that! You are a prisoner here. A killer who objects to my very existence, I know that. But let's see: this letter is very old, perhaps months old, and I think it must have gone through many hands before it reached the prison. Many carriers. And a lot of money. Hmm. We know someone who would like to speak with you about this letter."

We do not speak. I do not care what they want to know. I only know they will not get it from me.

The afternoon comes and goes and no one approaches the cell to take the bodies, which are now stinking beyond endurance. Flies light on the plaster like a black shroud, a seething mass, buzzing and vibrating with maddening zest, while Fady retreats to a corner and falls into a trance of prayer, mechanical and abstract, flowing like water over a wheel, over and over, on and on, the water flowing through the concrete trench, and his prayers flowing in the water. Several times a day, the water gushes down the sluice in a torrent. If there were only some way the other prisoners could learn of the bodies.

Three times the sewer has risen and emptied...that is how I know it is afternoon now. Perhaps around three o'clock. The next flush will be at six. Not yet dark. Could it be dark? The white flake of light about the door never changes. Time must be guessed at. I need to wait for the morning flush. Morning is the best time, better for my plan since more attention will be directed on the sewer at that time by the others. For the sluice runs best then. So I lie awake, thinking. When I suspect it is morning, having counted four more rises and falls of the sewer, I walk up to the bodies and test the hand of one. It is dry and crusted in the plaster, but having rotted in the heat, it gives loose to my touch and I see myself ripping off the hand, its bones cracking and giving way like the bones of a cooked chicken, and with a toss floating down the whorls of the sewer for others to discover.

I fear with a feverish half-mad fear of dying in this prison, our condition unknown to anyone. So again and again I see myself ripping off the hand, the bones cracking and with a splash disappearing under the wall where a babble of angry eruption seems to take place at the sight and discovery of the dismembered human part.

How long we have been waiting, then, is difficult to calculate. An hour. A day. Several days. Sometimes we receive food, but never at specific times. There is no order in the mind with time gone. Fady prays and chants. I begin to think of time in terms of chants. After 900 chants, an Arab trustee, a man with a leg so crippled he could never run away, shows his face with a creaking and slamming noise of the cell door. He brought a little water and a few pieces of fruit, but is very quiet about it, not speaking a word, then suddenly, looking into our faces so very intently we knew it was to warn us of something, the lips quickly say something like... *They know. They sent me to tell you they have seen your sign.*

But we have no time to mull over this brief exchange, for a regular platoon marches in behind the man, and in the opening doors down the corridor we can hear the screaming and ranting of the other prisoners calling out in a wild convulsion of rage: *Bodies! Bodies! Bodies!*

"Get out of here, you filthy pig!" one of the uniformed soldiers says to me, grabbing me by the hair and slinging me out into the corridor while he stands for a minute, as if hypnotized with horror, looking at the scattered parts of the corpses with white bones protruding from the sockets where the arms and feet have been pulled off.

"Disgusting pigs!" he shouts, shoving me in front of Fady, who has begun to weep aloud, giving thanks again to God for his freedom, for everyone's freedom, for our souls and for our bodies.

Hans and the American Father Town

FRAU ENGERS WAS LOOKING AT THE FACE OF HER SON. HE WAS seated on the expensive white sofa with his father's photographs spread before him on the table. She sat opposite him on a chaise longue, a delicate white-haired woman, half-covered in a blue silk eiderdown and holding a cup of tea in her hand. He came often to look at the album like this, and talk about this man, this American father he had never met.

The son was forty-two, unmarried. His mother was his only intimate. Intimate in the sense that they could spend hours together in stillness, a whole afternoon without the slightest fear of finding out some further thing in the other that might cause a quarrel or fight. For everything had already been found out, everything, years ago.

She could say what she wished to Hans; he gave her such freedom, such lovely peace, so that without guilt she repeated again, Sunday after Sunday, the endless story of her romance with his father, the American soldier stationed near Cologne in 1957. In the past, when Hans was a teenager, she was quick to put her hand on his, in a kind of proud surrender, and toss her head as if flinging tears back out of those fine, clear blue eyes, tears for dreams that had never materialized, dreams that can never come true, she would whisper.

She was a good talker, this little lady, her very soul full of that controlled, intense German energy which seemed to run without exertion out of her rather pretty, slight, and careful mouth. She was fascinated by herself, by her own past, her vigorous and burdensome heritage. Her mother had been from Cologne, but her father was Dutch and a prominent businessman. "Papa was caught behind the lines in Holland when Hitler's army rolled in and closed the borders...No one dared move in those days," she told him. "And we did not know for months if he was dead or alive. Then some boy got through to us. One of those couriers who made money carrying information by word of mouth to loved ones trapped inside the occupied countries. He always got his pay, you can be sure of that, for each word from him was like gold; we hung on his every word. It was he who told us how the Germans were treating the Dutch. They had gone from house to house in Amsterdam and ordered all the men to the street. The frail ones were sent in one direction; the more hardy ones were roped together and marched to a train headed for the labor camps. He saw my father, a very fastidious man who loved good clothes, like all his family, tied with a rope, being lead down the street with a lot of other men, all of them looking beaten, their heads hung down. I keep remembering that. My father, with his fine head, bowed, his hair falling. The Germans made them look to the ground as they walked.

"We waited for this courier, very anxious, like very sick people wait for a doctor. He was a good-looking boy, like you, Hans, and he and my mother were very friendly, you know. Later he helped my father file reparations orders against the German government. And we got a lot of money that way. Some of it went to my mother, who then divorced him, of course. For she was in love with the courier, the young handsome boy. Romance has never been far away from this family."

Hans stared at his mother. Now she was changing. Going downhill, her little feet sticking out under the blue cover were swollen around the ankles. He had believed she would become moribund and embarrassing with age. But something quite different had happened. She simply became puffed out and sleepy-looking, like a cat after it licks up all the cream from a bowl. And Hans felt she had licked his father all up; his father was disappearing like a bowl of milk. She was giving him up, letting him die, too lazy to keep summoning him back out of the faded-looking photographs. These days she finished off each conversation with the same tired irritability: "*Why don't you take the dog and go for a walk!*"

But now she lifted her head and put down her teacup.

"Ah, yes, your father was such a very handsome man!" she said again, a little breathless and roused. "All innocence in the American way of innocence. As if what they know they know only from their movies. What the movies teach them. Nothing else can reach them. So tall a man, and so proud of the world he came from...a little crazy dark place no one ever heard about — Scarletberry, West Virginia. Among the Appalachian Mountains where the men carried guns and vent hunting in the voods for rabbits and little strange animals the names of vich I can't remember. I think they even raced mules in the street. Or some such thing. Mule races! Yes. And there was this horrible old crumbling stone building, an insane asylum right in the middle of town. Fenced of course, because the place had a history, or what they called history. Each stone had been hand cut by slaves in the last century, which to them is very old history. 'Darkies,' I believe they call them. *Schwarzneger* who ran away when their Civil War happened. And the local people hunted them down in the hills with guns. Oh, they are all very proud of that, and everyone claims to be old slaveholders, wouldn't you know?

"So I learned a lot from their little newspaper. They have a little weekly rag sheet there that from time to time printed, and still prints, a picture of a lynching. It is a favorite of theirs. Verner would show me. 'Here,' he would say, 'this is the way it is in America.' Just to tease me, of course. And I would see this picture: A Negro body hanging from a bridge. What's that supposed to mean to me, I would ask, to a German? After all we've gone through, I ask you? I could never live there. It was not for me. So I told him. Go. My darling, please go and leave me.

"I am not anything like an American. I am a very cultured woman. Educated. A teacher. I have my life here. I like to dress up, you see that, Hans. With nice jewelry around my throat, and good silky dresses, and shoes. I like to go to the opera and stroll around in museums when the weather is damp and no good outside. My loyalty is to Cologne. I could never go waste away in some little coal cinder of a place like he lived in. It would be a death worse than any bridge death I could imagine. I would rather be some *Schwarzneger* hanging by his neck from the bridge, I tell. So what can I say? Here is a picture of the two of us standing beneath the cathedral, the great spiral catching the sun like it is a rocket exploding against the sky.

"Maybe he knew about you, Hans, maybe not. I forget. I'm getting old. I think I told him, but he was a busy man. What does it matter? He went back home and went into politics." His mother's accent grew thick at times with tension. He could feel her tension rise and fall. "They elected him something or other in this town. Mayor. Yes, mayor of that little town. And we wrote each other a lot of letters, then we didn't write so often. I don't know. We forgot about each other. Sometimes he would send a local newspaper with his picture in it, him officiating at some function. Moose Clubs and Little League games. That kind of deadly stuff. I would look at these photographs and think, *Oh, my God, how, how, how did we ever become connected, a great old city like Cologne, a Roman settlement since 50 A.D. and all those miserable American army people? Flooding Germany.* History is too cruel to the heart. I don't want to talk about it anymore, Hans. I'm very weak today. Why don't you take the dog and go for a walk."

So he took the dog and went out, down the boulevard with a wind beginning to blow from the dock side of the river. A type of anguish was beginning in him, a kind of weight creeping up around his heart with such sharpness he almost cried out. He did in fact catch his breath in such a strange way that it made the dog look around at him. The melancholy had not happened all at once, but had been growing all day and had to do with his mother's swollen ankles and the whiteness around her eyes, an ugly slow decay setting in. Always decay. Nothing could stop it. The only way to escape it was to never have existed. So decay was a privilege. He swung his head and turned down his mouth and noticed an old woman staring at him. The very privileged misery of living and dying. What if he had missed this anguish? What if he had never been born? Never got to see all this?

The old woman sat across from him on a bench. She was bundled up in the wind with dark, heavy clothing; stockings and shoes; a small shriveled face like a heap of raked leaves, waiting for him to do something strange. *Even she at one time had been someone's baby*, he thought in the cold gloom with a hint of a smile. A hundred years ago someone had brushed her bald head and stared with love into her face. It was all so monstrous, so monstrous to be thinking this way. He ran his hand over his eyes, which he thought were full of tears, but were dry and beginning to ache.

His mind went back to his father, a naïve man from a shabby, naïve background somewhere in a benighted America. Jokes were made about the people where his father came from. It was all prejudice, but prejudice did not live without its long, malignant root in truth, sipping and growing. He knew that. Yet there — there in such a town, Hans himself existed! The thought suddenly astounded him. That he should exist somewhere in the minds of a town. Hans as a rumor. People imagining him from time to time. He had flowed into their talk and thoughts. It was fascinating. His mother's love letters had of course been passed around to certain people there, discussed with roused fascination. And if he called there? Called the local editor of that newspaper? His very name would cause excitement. It was as if he existed in two places at the same time. Two lives.

He began to humor himself more and more; he pulled on the dog's leash to continue the walk. The street was very noisy. All kinds of traffic: new, shiny, colorful cars like a jungle of birds stirring. And there was a religious procession underway, so he thought it must be Mardi Gras. Yes, Mardi Gras. But he paid so little attention to what happened on the ground. For he was a pilot, and his thoughts, like the birds, were always on the world above, in the sky. It was the weather that concerned him. Not the Mardi Gras procession. The weather and the clouds, the rising storm clouds. His ears were to the weather, his very skin listened for rain.

Of course he had been to the United States hundreds of times. For he was an airline pilot. He had even been to

Pittsburgh many times, which was within driving miles of this father who dominated so much of his thinking, but he had never until this day felt the exertion of his father's blood pull him to the countryside. Only now had the idea of actually seeing his father in the flesh come to him.

He flew for a well-known German airline, and this made him very proud. And it made him see things in a very special way. His eyes could detect something out of line in a second. A pilot must, or you know what would happen. He was always seeing to things, straightening things. A crooked lampshade in a room drove him mad. Shoes must be placed close together, ready to go. So didn't it make a tidy sense to go see his father? Keep his life in line? A pilot kept everything lined up, in order. He was an excellent pilot. Everything had to be straight. One mistake and you knew what would happen to you, Hans, no matter how beautiful your blond German hair.

And he loved the air. He loved the joking men he flew with. They knew about his birth. Pilot error, they laughed with him, and you're not the only one, Hans! Still, they treated him a little differently. He could feel that they were protective of him somehow, sensing that underneath he felt an emptiness, and had not married. Had no wife. They would go with him to see his father. They would not let him go alone. He adored his friends Klaus and Oskar and Egon.

When Hans walked the dog back to his mother, he patted her like a tame goose. The excitement of his plan was flapping like mad in his mind. He would not tell her yet. But less than a week later he and his friends went off together to West Virginia. They had flown to Pittsburgh and rented a car; now they were headed down Interstate 79, still laughing from the drunken party of the night before where they had women and dressed up in silly hillbilly costumes, blacked their teeth. Sang songs. And told jokes about hill people. *Ah, who made up such twisted little thoughts*, he wondered. Those sudden little hate bombs of delight. This was how the secret malice of the world was passed around, really, with wild intimate laughter, these jokes like rude supports under a kind of squirming hate. Let me tell you this one. Why did the hillbilly take a box of tampons to prison with him? They were still laughing when they got into the small town.

It was late afternoon, the early part of March. The cold was gone, but warm weather had not arrived. They had been on the interstate two and a half hours when they came to their exit.

There followed several introductory miles of the usual fast food places, a shopping mall and some gas stations; then the street narrowed and the town expressed itself. A dim greyish light fell over everything like a depression. *Welcome to Scarletberry, W.Va. Home of Buck Latimore. The Singing Humanitarian.*

They drove around looking for a motel, talking with great excitement, wondering how the town would react to the news of a former mayor's indiscretion showing up in the flesh. It would cause a big commotion, they were certain. But perhaps Hans should stay out of sight for a few days. Perhaps he should call a press conference, with the town's dignitaries or give a private interview to the local news. People had no doubt argued about the affair for years, until it was a sort of legend.

Wilson Goodloe stood in the tall windows of his bank in Scarletberry and looked absently down the main street. Out of the glare of the setting sun he watched the bright chromium grill-work of a strange car approach up the hill and pass in front of him. It was a large Audi with four men in it, laughing and having a good time. The one in the front passenger seat looked like he had his hair dyed yellow. The car crossed the intersection and drove out of sight around the corner. "That's him," Goodloe said to himself without any excitement of thought or feeling.

That morning he had received a call from the town clerk's office informing him of a call from a Pittsburgh attorney who represented a certain Hans Engers, a young man claiming to be Werner Heffner's son by a German woman from days gone by. Heffner had died ten days ago and was buried without fanfare in the local cemetery. Goodloe's bank was trustee to the estate. If it was money the young man was after, Goodloe could tell him to save his gas and mileage. There wasn't any.

Goodloe was a busy man. As the wealthy owner of the biggest bank in town (an impressive architectural structure built by his family on foreclosed land mortgages after the collapse of 1929), he was protected from all surprises and shocks in this world by a tight little network of sharp listeners. He was the same Goodloe who made national news a few years ago when he threw a man out of the bank for carrying mud in on his shoes. Had the client arrested for destruction of bank property and his account closed out. "And don't you never, never come back in here again!" was his last finger pointing address to the man.

Very few outsiders could add anything to Goodloe's life. The place to comment on his bad grammar or his white polished tennis shoes was the place your luck ran out in that town. He wondered what Heffner's son thought he could tell people around here, that love could buy you money?

The motel our German pilots picked was being used by a swarm of hunters that weekend. Rough-looking men milling around in paramilitary garb with slain deer strapped to the tops of cars in the parking lots. The animals had a human quality to them somehow, like slender people prepared for autopsies. Or for strange burials where their entrails were scraped out.

In the noisy lounge Hans and his friends began to drink with them in a formal, reserved manner, but once they had a few more drinks, a meanness rose between the two groups. It was Oskar who began to slyly make insinuating remarks about the town. "Because I read on the box you can go horseback riding, swimming and play tennis with them. See? And I hear you strung up some *Schwarzneger* here at one time," he began, "From the town bridge. There's a picture around. I've heard about it. Even in Germany we have heard about that photograph. And I would like to have a copy of the original if I might. I would pay big money for it. Nothing would be considered over my head, as long as it was within reason, of course. And I understand you once had a mayor here who was quite a lady's man, right? What was his name, huh? "

No one knew what the visitors were talking about. Or they pretended not to know. The hunters claimed they were from out of town; they had never been to this part of the mountains before. But they had been to Germany. Stationed there in the military, they said. Something they would never forget, for the place was crawling with crazy wild women, the kind who really knew how to take care of a man with a dollar bill in his pocket. They would reach you a drink in one hand and a sweat band in the other, then they'd break your back for the next ten hours. God, did the men around here need the military in those days.

The fight began in the bar and worked its way into the hall with loud curses, grunts, and body slams. From there, it pitched and tumbled out into the parking lot. Off in the distance the police sirens began. Hans was knocked to the ground and kicked. Oscar was punched and dragged by the hair. But Klaus managed to get to the car and drive them out of there before the police arrived. They felt lucky to get away, out of the town and back onto the thruway, that great stretch of road like an international reserve where they felt safe. What on earth had they been thinking about? Coming down here among a bunch of ignorant hicks who would just as soon shoot you as say hello? They began to laugh at what had happened. Why were they acting like this, like a bunch of slumming teenagers? Bumming around? Yet it was wonderful somehow as well. "Did you hear when that one son of a bitch said, '*Cologne? That's where Nietzsche caught syphilis, right?*' How would he know something like that?" It was amazing. And very exciting, except Hans now was very silent; his handsome exquisite face showed stress, as if he was in great pain. "It's my leg," he told them. "I can't bear my leg any longer. I need to have you turn the car around. I want to go back to the hospital. Back to the town."

"Back to the town? Tell me you can't be serious; tell me you can't mean it? Back there? Tell me I didn't hear right!"

But Hans began to scream in agony until, frightened, his friend turned off at the next exit that showed among its signs the blue hospital logo of a stick man lying in a bed. "You go on to Pittsburgh," he told them once they reached the emergency room in Scarletberry. "I'll keep in touch."

There was no talking to Hans now. Standing on his good leg, his face distorted into a mass of misery, he waved them on.

"But don't you think we should wait with you? To see if anything is wrong?

"Of course something is wrong. My leg is broken. I can tell that. You go on, get some sleep before your flights takes off."

So they left him, staring after his disappearing shape between the wide, spreading doors. An attendant had come sleepily out and put him in a wheelchair and wheeled him away, his blond head lying back in pain. There was nothing to do but leave him.

His leg was indeed broken. The bone shattered. A specialist had to be called in to do surgery. Hans was very much taken by this little hospital, The General. So clean and tidy, with bright banks of forsythia budding outside the window on the hillside. There was almost no noise, the place was so small. Now and then he could hear a lot of female voices. Nurses breaking out laughing. Everyone seemed to laugh too much, to make up for the lack of words. Out of all these voices and footsteps someone was bound to open his door. A huge laughing face screaming his name...no... a small, tiny face whispering. "*So, it is you, Hans Heffner? You have come to us at last. We knew you would come one day.*"

Now he could think with a clearer mind. His friends had put him off to such a bad start. They were a mistake and a disaster. They could not possibly understand the significance of this event. This event he had been approaching all his life. How could anyone understand it? He lay with his leg elevated, waiting. Ah, what is going to happen to you, Hans, in this little, soulless town?

At last the door swung open and the doctor came to see him. Dr. Whitehurst.

Whitehurst was a grey-haired man with a tanned, blade-like face, a dignified authority figure worthy perhaps even of Han's secrets and confidences. Hans shook hands with him and asked if he was from this town.

"Why, yes. I know it's hard to believe. A hometown doctor that's not Arab or Filipino — I tell you, we're used to foreigners here." They talked for a few minutes. "You don't know who I am?" Hans said cautiously.

The doctor was taken up short. He looked quickly at the patient. Of course the accent was strange. "Verner Heffner? Do you know Mayor Verner Heffner?" Hans almost whispered.

"I did know him." the doctor said frankly, but rather off-handed. "He's dead now. Died just a couple of weeks ago. In fact he died right here in this very room. In the same bed you're lying on."

Hans stared at him; fear rose in his face at the doctor's sudden and unexpected words, at the bizarre thought of lying in his father's deathbed. Was it really here, where his own body pressed against the mattress, that his father had met the sting of death? "Are you sure? Are you sure? In this bed? That's remarkable."

"What's so remarkable about it? Many people have died in that bed. Most of them my patients, too, ha ha, but we always remove the mattresses. Give them to the state prison. What might be your interest in Werner?"

"Verner was my father."

"Father?" The doctor pulled the sheet back from Hans's leg and stared at his bruised flesh. He listened to Hans without taking his eyes off the leg as if echoes of Werner were flying out of the depths of the raw, bluish and waterlogged wound. Hans was saying, "No, not married. They never married. And it was a terror of mine as a child that I might meet him one day. When I was a boy, I was afraid of meeting him. Then I grew up and the terror disappeared. My vision straightened out. I became a man. I flew an airplane. Suddenly I was no longer afraid and I wanted to see him. Just once. I wanted to meet him and tell him how I knew all about him. I wanted to tell him how I had come to love him. I wanted —" he reached for a glass of water and the doctor lifted his eyes. The manner of the man was very theatrical and childish. But offensive in some way, too, like a haughty child who wants to give orders.

And again the doctor was not accustomed to hearing people talk intimately about themselves, and he felt uneasy in the young man's presence. He wondered what this bird really wanted.

"I'll need someone to show me his gravesite. That's about all," he explained. His eyes were steady and coldly scrupulous. The doctor thought it very strange the son did not inquire as to the cause of his father's death. It was alcoholism.

"Well, that will take some time. For now, you must stay off this leg, God damn it. Unless you want to lose it. It was a long surgery, you know. Sixteen hours in all. You didn't take it as well as I thought you would. You drink a little? Liquor's not good for you. But if you just turn your head and look out the window, you can see the little cemetery where your daddy is sleeping. Up there on the hill among those pines and blooms. I understand how you are longing to go and see his grave. 'Cause we only get one daddy, don't we?"

Hans turned his head and looked away, as if to hide a smirk of a smile on his lips from the doctor's simple-minded manner as he tried to console him. It was all so quaint, so sweet. This must be what his mother had meant by their innocence. He must call her and tell her he had made contact with the town at last.

Part II

Keeping notes for Klaus and Oskar during the day, so I can write them later. Told them I would write, so I am doing it. Left the hospital for a small room in a private nursing home. All day make the notes out of this strange world I have landed in. Have come to one conclusion: It doesn't take much to make a person feel alone. Make him drink or eat just one little thing he is not accustomed to, and instantly he is in the darkest outreaches of another existence. That's the way people are. So imagine how I must feel, a kraut to the bone, forced even to drink their hideous weak beer and eat their good home cooking with plenty of ass crumbs and little roach wings floating in every dish — and you can guess at my isolation.

The leg is mending quite well, by the way, in spite of the beans and cornbread, and phony pizza and stale salad plates.

My father is dead, and who can blame him? Look at this place! Called my mother with the news. Called and called and finally she answered. By then I had half-forgotten what I wanted to say. She was so still, so silent at my voice, and then I heard the tiny, tiny sniffling.

I say I am alone, but I know I am being watched. From all corners their eyes are on me.

This morning I woke to find a man standing just outside my room. A murmurous shadow with its head bowed, and then, as if on cue, the head jerked up and in three fell swoops he was next to me with his hand raised, his eyes shut tight, and began to pray for the peace and serenity of one sent among them — the issue of a brother who had gone out to fight for his country and serve his country's name, only to fall between the corrupt flesh of a loveless woman. Couldn't guess who that was. But the prayer continued in its long and tender endeavor until the chaplain (or whatever he was) opened his eyes to see me gawking at him in amused delight. My hair sticking up around my head like dead weeds. He was much taken aback by my rudeness, but then went on to say by way of explanation that this was simply his job. He was paid to do for God (with resentment accumulating in his large frigid eyes) what God could not bear do for himself. So I had to take that! Still thinking that over. Ha ha.

So my father is dead. Barely cold when I got here. Imagine such luck! So I must go out and find him in the people themselves. As he existed among them.

Discharged from the nursing facility this morning and took my first real ride around the town. Hired a driver. Stood on the ugly, grey, little main street. Not a soul in sight. Several drab women, with long stringy hair, in flat-heeled men's shoes with white anklets. Carrying loaded shopping bags in both hands. Went past me without looking. Not even a glance, although I was dressed in my pilot's uniform and stuck out like I was in neon Technicolor against the leaden background.

Stood looking in the plate glass windows of a store front, when I noticed a large car carrying a little bald-headed man, then it came back, passed me several times. The same little man who stands in front of the bank like he owns it, his polished tennis shoes glowing. He is obviously watching me for some reason. Did not nod or wave in response to my lifting my chin, very slightly to be sure. Trucks. Convoys of drilling rigs. What can they think when they see me? Quietly they keep their heads averted but I can feel them staring, feel their minds working me over. I keep a smile ready just in case they want to make contact.

For the last few days have made a quick intense study of town society. Found it is run by a snobbish, jealous little in-group, very much determined that no outsiders are coming in here to show them anything new, which would be unbearable, no doubt about it. I suspect I have united them further by giving them something to talk about. How can they possibly avoid me? When I walk around the streets dressed in my immaculate uniform. I am very tall compared to them. And very blond, of course. While they tend to be short and stubby, although some of the women might be very good-looking were it not for the prevalence of that long Scots-Irish jaw showing up everywhere you look that long-of-jaw, short-of-thigh trait. My God, there are moments of such acute repugnance for these faces...the likes of which might make up a good part of my own genetic material, that a panic rushes upon me, and with such alarm I actually feel I want to castrate myself right on the spot to save the world from further ugliness. But these rushes do not last very long, and I comfort myself with a good, harsh, German cigarette, smoked down to my fingertips, and then flipped into the muddy water of the slow, weed-choked river.

Today I have moved from a cramped little room near the hospital to private quarters on a hill overlooking the better part of the town. "Very beautiful," the nurse chimed. "Maybe it will remind you of Germany." She is very polite, but oh-so-gross. I do mean *gross*. I can hear her panting miles away, climbing the steps, while I run ahead of her, even though I am on crutches. Very busy. Very excited. She leaves me to go down into the town for food. If she eats anything except Thrill Food it is a great depravation in her eyes. Must have her Thrill Burgers! Her Thrill Fries! I look at her large breasts with mild pity. She has several like-sized friends who come walking towards me like a city on legs.

I must get in new furniture, for, although people are slow about it, I know word is out, and that they will be coming to see me. When I appear in the streets, it is always with a face prepared to receive even the sleepiest gaze, and to ignore all those other little pretenses of indifference they are so skilled at using, as if nothing could stir them. But I know their ears are up. And I must behave just right, must make the apartment reflect the special image of how I live away from here, in a colorful and urbane dignity.

Sofa removed and new one carried up the hill. Fine silky white sofa and some Queen Anne chairs. Nice little front porch; under the stars at night faraway dogs bark. Nurse comes twice a week to see to my leg and to run the sweeper and bring what I want from the stores. Cleaning lady hired. Hired another driver. A mere kid who asked me if they have fraternities in Germany. He says proudly that he belongs to one at the college he attends. "We're real animals," he says, and I look at him, his small nervous hands and flat round eyes. A marmoset is the animal he resembles. Still on crutches for several more weeks. Everything ready, yet not a soul comes to the door. The phone does not ring. Lucky mother warned me how reclusive these hill people can be. Decided to place an ad in the newspaper. That will break the ice.

Hans Engers Is at Home at 10 Hilly Uplands to Receive Visitors and Relatives with Information on his Father and Late Mayor Werner Heffner. Interested persons may call between hours of 10:00 A.M. and 8:00 P.M. 269-4266.

Waited eagerly all day for the phone to ring. Waited eagerly for the mailman. Listened intently and nervously for footsteps, for the little dog in the next apartment to bark, but all is silent. The rain is silent, falling silently. Town below shrouded in mist. Chill mornings. The population itself has disappeared from the face of the earth, as if swallowed up inside Wal-Mart, or one of the other the great, deadly-looking shopping malls off the interstate. Obviously they are going out of their way to ignore me. They are in this together. Even the cleaning lady is cunning, sly and evasive: *Honey, I couldn't even tell you who the present mayor is, let alone one twenty years ago.*

But they won't get away with any little tricks against me. Let my lawyers in Pittsburgh know what they are trying to pull, and we went into City Hall this morning to take possession of my father's estate. The clerk at the desk pretended shock and dismay when we asked for the house keys, her round eyes opened larger and larger until I thought her head would split . "But, but," she said in that babyish drawl they have, "you can't just go looking around his house. How do we know you're really Werner Heffner's son? We can't open up his possessions to you. Not just anybody can start pawing through his belongings, his things. You'll have to get a court order for that. Anyone should know that," and she looked at my lawyer. "But before a court order, you'll have to establish paternity. I don't want to be unkind, but I hope you understand that this is a legal matter. And that he never married. Heffner was a bachelor. But there are relatives. Other relatives that must be considered."

I looked at the little bug-eyed wench as if she must be mad. "*Of course my father never married!*" I told her in a whisper that nearly broke my teeth with its hiss. He was in love with my mother. How could she be so ignorant of what went on in this town? She drew back as if she had opened a drawer on a rat and couldn't slam it shut again. We stared at each other.

And as for the relatives, I had heard from them this very morning. I began to smile as I took the note out of my pocket and showed her. It was handwritten on a dirty piece of notebook paper. I know you are one of us. I can tell you have our blood in you. Make them dig your father up and test his corpse. Make them take his leg and place it against yours. I think it would prove you got your bad leg from your father. He always did have trouble with that leg. Varicose veins and blood clots. Make them take his left leg.

"But...this is not enough to establish paternity," the girl informed me, handing back the note, her enraged face causing me to laugh so loud I nearly doubled up on the floor.

Going back and forth to Pittsburgh now to consult with specialists. But am aware of the note the whole time. Keep it in my pocket, but take it out and read it while bursting out laughing, right in traffic. Sent copy to Oskar and Egon. As for the lawyer, he is very good. Thinks nothing of sitting up half the night over drinks, discussing the case. It was a very wise move on my part to hire him, someone from out of town. For no one here can be trusted to tell me the truth. They are fighting me at every turn. Obviously my father has money somewhere. Perhaps hidden in the old shabby house they will not allow me to enter.

The house is quite near, a weathered little clapboard on the hillside with lopsided steps leading up. Slippery wet path. The windows bare. Naked. Like human eyes smeared over with some kind of queer oily medication that makes them sightless. Pressing my face to the panes, I could see someone is using the rooms as recycling bins to store mountains of old bottles of all colors and shapes.

And there is a dog house where a dog has been; the grass is still worn off in a circle around it. Worn into nothingness. And then...

Wondering what happened to the dog. Perhaps it is the same one that barks all the time from the next apartment. Absurdly, I stare at this dog when I pass it now and try to talk to it, a grey and white Springer that is very friendly and wags its stump of a tail. "Have you had the dog long?" I asked its owner, a little plump boy with a red-stained mouth, who stared and did not answer. "Did someone give you that dog?" I heard myself shouting as he turned and ran off. A woman came to the window and looked down at me suspiciously. I lifted my hand in a sort of corrupted salute, a fluttering motion of my fingers. The woman did not smile. Must be more careful. Nerves could send me out of control in a second.

The days run on. The chill spring rains are endless. Silent foggy nights. Dew-laden mornings. Went prowling around the town in my long storm coat, looking for clues to Father, whose presence I feel everywhere in the wind that sweeps in over the lush, spring-roused hills. Toured the old psychiatric hospital alone without my driver. Alone. Large misanthropic place. Lobotomy rooms with great worn tables. Torture chambers. Hallways so large they have their own weather patterns. Light fog stirred around my feet, water dripping in the basement rooms. Been empty now for twenty years. Teenagers ride their motorcycles in the great hallways at night, bats and pigeons fluttering about the tall windows, several derelicts crawling out of sight. Yet here my father worked. Had a job as maintenance man. Walked, walked about thinking of my mother. Wanting my mother. My heart fluttering, pounding. Here in this desolation fell my babyish footsteps, racing towards my father, my babyish cries that made him turn in the night as he slept under the courthouse tower striking the hours over the town. I hear it still, striking the hours in the misty air, under the great moon, mingled with voices along the dark thickets of the riverbank. I wake and turn, my arms reaching...woke this morning with a dry mouth and cramps. Drank several bottles of beer to wash my guts. Beer tastes better than at first.

Made my way to the local tavern. Why didn't I think of this sooner? Place filled with men who knew my father. They almost fell all over me, buying me drinks and laughing at stories about my father whom they all admired. Stumbled home at three in the morning. Couldn't get up the long steps so I slept on the grass.

The new nurse, a woman past middle age, looks at me squarely, and speaks so primly only a speck of pink light shows in her dark round face as she opens her lips. I catch her staring at my hair, and later plucking a few bright strands from my brush, curiously touching it with a sulk on her mouth as if finding out I might be putting something on it. "That's where your father slept half the time," she said in reference to the grass. "He didn't get along with a lot of people. This here's a Christian town. When a lot of people tried to close the bars he fought that," she said. I laughed in her face with pride for my father, who endured such minds. Went out and bought a six-pack in his honor. Decided to go back to the tavern. It was nearly empty, being a slow weekday evening. Nevertheless I waited around until closing and again had to sleep on the grass at the foot of the steps.

Now news of my paternity case is in the little newspaper. At last a little attention. At last they can no longer pretend there is nothing between me and the town.

That for forty years my shadow has not extended itself over this place, and now it rises, physically crosses their very vision so they must lift their eyes and look. Ah, look!

A fine close-up shot in color on the front page. The deep blue of my pilot's uniform contrasting strongly with my yellow hair. Maybe a little garish, maybe reminiscent of those old German Youth posters that are worth a fortune these days. Those expensive side jabs from the old, insane past. Yet there is something weak about me as well. Or is that imagined? Something over-awed and rapt, which at times gives a certain uneasy feeling that, with one push from behind, I would go soaring and screaming against the sky in slobbering terror. No, that is just my mind playing around with itself. Perhaps to save itself from...what? What is after my mind? When actually I am very tough, filled with a hard and pushing spirit that never rests.

Sat watching my interview on television. I could see my strength come forth. I am striking, very good-looking, I admit. My slow accent, my mouth forming the American words is charming. To watch me is to watch a bit of strange provocative theater. I sat in the dark, in the audience, seeing a man with a cool aloofness, a lofty importance, as if he were an apocalyptic creature, like something out of the Bible, pulling a whole town into his life of sorrow. I wept for the man. I forgot who he was and I jumped up and began to pace about in my room, pacing up and down on my crutches. Wondering what was going to happen to him. That man. Couldn't sleep. Drank several bottles of warm beer before falling into a stupor.

Sought out the town's newspaper editor in his office this morning. Head aching. Asked him to have a drink with me. I had a bottle in my briefcase and he jumped up like he was in great danger. As if someone had begun to strip off their clothes in front of him. Ha! What a fool. I only wanted to show him some special photographs, but he placed them aside with hardly a glance and took out some of his own. An enormous stack that he kept in a walk-in safe. I prepared myself. These, I quietly conjectured, were old photographs of my father, the former mayor. He had been waiting for the right moment to show them to me.

But it turned out they were only shots of the editor himself, who had been a basketball star in high school. He had made more rebound shots than anyone who had ever played for the town. And more hook shots. And more free shots. He had scored sixty-three points in the famous game against Milford Hills. The town went crazy, he told me. He married the Homecoming Queen. They have three children. Three oval-framed pictures on his desk of three little long-jawed girls. Can any bottle of liquor be worse than that?

I tried to talk to him about my mother then. I broke open several of my father's letters about the town, descriptions of the landscapes of the town, the river, the court house, the old jail, the asylum which was crumbling even then. I wanted him to see that I felt I belonged to this place. I wanted the editor to print the letters. He took the packet I held out to him without speaking. He looked insulted, as if he were being overshadowed. Which he was, of course, but that's no fault of mine. And then I dropped the real bomb. The letter in which my father told my mother twenty years ago who was taking bribes in the bank. I show the editor the letter and he pretended it was nothing. I repeated the name. Isn't that a relative of Mr. Goodloe? I asked him. Perhaps his own father?

Monday morning. A registered letter from my attorneys. Some good news at last!

Exhumation has been scheduled. The town sexton's ready. Father's thigh bone is to be taken and sent to a famous laboratory for testing against blood and hair samples I have provided. Wrote Mother. Want her present at the event. For father must be given a proper funeral with hymns and music when the grave is re-closed. Call Mother often, sometimes several times a day. Faxed her copies of the interviews, as well as the photographs of me in the little newspaper father mentioned so often. Did not these photographs spread across the front page prove the town has taken me to its bosom? She sounds surprised. Gasping for breath at times at my courage. But did she actually think her only son would allow their lives to pass like music no one wanted to listen to any longer?

Clothes for the exhumation laid out. I shall wear a pilot's cape. Long and dark, swooping around my boots. Bareheaded in the wind. Mother with similar dark cape, darkish red in color with a white lily in her hand. Also in shiny boots. The hired photographer and the hymn singers following discretely. They will sing "I've Been Looking for a Home." It is not an old song, but one I wrote myself. Copies to be handed out to all the press.

Problems. New trouble. Judge won't let us proceed. Judge pretending outrage at "the mayor's old girlfriend," as he refers to my mother. Trying to keep her out of the picture. Judge belongs to that same haughty little group of Big Bodies that includes Tennis Shoe Goodloe, who has fallen in love with me, it seems. Can't get me off his mind. Follows me around the streets, reflecting like a phantom out of the shop windows when I stop to look. He is the one who wrote to the newspaper — or caused someone to write — a suggestion that the city of Cologne purchase the old asylum and turn it into a love letter museum. That's what he considers humor, the little sick, nasty bird doing its droppings.

Now guess what? Old Goodloe's father, the one with the poison paw, has shot himself in the head. Everyone is saying he secretly had prostate cancer. In the bar a man took a long swallow of beer and said, "That's what you get for being an old buck." But I know and Tennis Shoe Goodloe knows no one shoots himself over prostate, a rather ubiquitous condition in old bucks. Cancer can't go where I go: deep into the secret bowels of shame. The old thief!

Back in court. Stood before the judge with my lawyers to plead for my mother's presence. I squared my shoulders as if against all the suffering I had endured in this life. An intense look on my face, hollow-eyed, but smiling slightly before speaking, as if musing. Knowing I was very pale. A pale light in the waiting room. They carried me home three times this week. Three times they let me sleep in the rain. Chest congested. Cough very bad. Then asked the judge to think how accidental all life is. He said he had already thought about that. "Think about it," I repeated as if I did not hear him. "What if we, each of us, had missed all this?" And my face opened then with a smile that was like an intrusion, like a door slowly opening into the sleeping dark where they all lay. "Whatever we have in this world that is worthwhile," I continued, "we get from women. Let no one tell you otherwise. So I must have my mother beside me when my father is touched again by earthly hands."

Room crowded with spectators, strangers of course, media people. Now I sprang my real secret. The one I had been keeping in my pocket. I announced I would run for mayor in the forthcoming election. I thought it would be a fitting end to my struggle. I should love to be mayor of my father's town. In this way the two of us would be united by the people themselves, our two souls could pass untouched into one life.

Judge very angry. Made accusations. Something about turning this town into a
circus. "I thought it already was a circus!" someone yelled, snickering in a vile, loud noise through his nose, and security had to be called in to quiet the crowd.

At last the storm begins to release itself! I am someone who jabs them out of their unconscious stupor they call existence. I am a pair of low-beating wings. All this clumsy hometown stuff is becoming very, very nauseating to me. The people all have body odor, I now notice. All these bodies like fat gleaners. Fat storage tanks. All the fat in nature will disappear into coffins, locked underground with them. What a contribution they are making to nature! Yet they need someone like me to expose their ugliness to the light. To make them pay attention to time. To impose order. I will do many things for them when I am elected. I dream of change for them, change that is heavily rolling and ripping, tearing into a new age. I will sit in City Hall with the wind lashing down the river, rain falling against the old buildings, my secretaries and commissioners listening to my ideas that heave and widen in the room.

"You're piling up on me!" That's what she said. That little clerk with the popcorn eyes. "Piling up." What an expression. She said this when I objected to the registration fee that must be paid for being on the ballot. She put her fingers on the counter and made them go, like horses galloping. *Hans-Engers-Hans-Engers-Hans-Engers* she kept repeating, as if trying not to lose her little temper. Piling up. That made me laugh.

Very good spirits. Everything going fine. Spent several hours in the bars with my father's old buddies. But when I emerged, I saw Wilson Tennis Shoe Goodloe looking from the end of the street, peeping around the corner. I ran towards him on my crutches, fast, which startled the crap out of him, causing him to turn rump and run like he was shitting bricks for the China wall.

Oh, Klaus, you must, must come to me at once. Something very terribly American has happened to me. Too American to repeat just now. But don't let Mother hear a word! I can't tell you how badly handled your friend has been. Oh, what a bunch of Nazis run these little American towns. How they pretend to be democratic and care for the rights of men. Good Lord, here they came and asked abruptly to see my identifications. Right on the street. As if I were a mere tourist. "If your name is Hans Engers," they said, "you've got no business in Scarletberry, West Virginia this fine morning. Not with an expired visa."

So I was handcuffed and frisked. Shoved around. They told me to shut up my mouth when I started to protest. But I didn't go meekly, I tell you. I fought them until I was half-dead from exhaustion, so they had to get a straitjacket, bind my arms to my side and stick a dirty filthy rag in my mouth. My eyes rolled around. And there was Goodloe, watching me with that bullfrog face of his. They drove me here to this airport where I remain in special custody. You must come as soon as you receive this!

Oskar, what has happened to Klaus? Why don't you come! One of you. I beg you, do something! Am I to stay at the mercy of these brutal immigration officials forever? Today I announced my hunger strike, and at the same time placed an ad in the paper for a wife. With a wife they cannot force me out of the country. Already I have lost twenty pounds. My clothes are bagging off me. I can hardly hold my poor head up long enough to comb my hair, which looks like a flattened gold crown, and not one word from any of you. Where is my mother? What's this crap about her forgetting who I am? Her only son? How can that be? If only I had a drink! One little bottle of beer! But all I get is some talk about the DTs. "You have the DTs," they keep telling me.

"What in holy hell are the DT's?" I scream, realizing suddenly it is a new species of lice. For I could feel them crawling all over me, eating out my ears and eyes, making a dry, hard, chewing sound. I screamed until my throat ran bloody water. And clawed my eyes and ears half out of my head. Then I grew calm. I don't know how many days I have been here.

Never mind coming to see me. I don't care if you ever speak my name again. Today I learned to my surprise that I am still on the ballot for the mayor's race! They cannot force me off without a trial, and a trial will take months yet. So what if I win the election? Whatever will they do? Ha ha ha!

My spirits are up again at last. And now this morning two women who claim to be my cousins arrived. They are bright-faced, good-hearted girls who tried before to befriend me but I was too busy at the time. Now they are very shy around me, but want to know me. They want to love me, they say. And brought me presents. Stationery and stamps. And a little pound cake they made themselves. "To break your fast on," they laughed, cutting a small piece and holding it to my lips so I could take a nibble. I think they were ready to chew it for me if needed.

"Oh, it is nothing." they said. "You are kin. You are supposed to be treated this way. And we just want you to know we feel your pain. We are sorry the world has to be the way it is. So full of traps!"

And yet it leaves me angry. The pride they feel helping someone down on his knees, the thrill of lifting me shows in their eyes. The shrewd, quaint insult in it. An insult I had to submerge the moment they stood and held out their arms to me as they were ready to leave. I bent forward and embraced them, holding their warm bodies close as if to receive the love so long denied me. Yet I wanted to say, “Turn loose of me with your young, warm arms. What do you think you are doing to me?” But they had such strength I could not push them away.

Disgust

FROM INSIDE THE WALLED GARDEN, THE GIRL COULD HEAR the opening sounds of the fine sunny May morning. Church had just let out, and people were coming across the old city park amid the ringing bells, shouting laughter and running barking dogs. Yet true spring was a good month away and misty, soot-crusted snow still lay in icy patches beneath the recesses of hedges and benches that bordered the large mansions around the park.

In her short summery skirt the girl was briskly setting up tables for guests. For a garden party. She covered each of the tables with a heavy, white lace cloth, then folded a clear plastic cover over the cloth and anchored the center with a vase of water into which she pushed sprigs of lilac and carnations. She kept looking up at the sky as if she did not quite trust all the bright openness, as if she expected storm clouds to come rolling in off the harbor and spoil everything with tearing gusts of wind and rain.

The timeless winters in this northern lakeshore region caused such unease, forced people to tighten up as they stepped out into the air, so that even in the bright summer sun there was about them this vague never-warmed look, as if the snows had recessed only to the edge of town and there waited like a ghostly glacier, from which a cold wind crept down and around their bare necks.

This past winter had been too severe. It was winters like that which made life a closed book so much of the time, shutting people inside, into themselves. So that with all this sudden warmth, so bright and abrupt, the human system was shocked, as with little cold, quick rinses of light deep in the nerves where no one could see, where thoughts flickered as if in a high thawing air, then fell, then darted away again out of their own eddying, like wild geese in the breaking emerald blue ice of the harbor below. "Wild Geese," the girl said out of nowhere, her lips parting. *Wild Geese*. Was there a song about wild geese? A very old forgotten song? "My heart knows what the wild goose knows." Somewhere a song like that. Wild goose. Brother goose. That was it. "*Wild goose, brother goose, which is best?* A wandering foot or a heart at rest?"

She arranged the flowers carefully, snipping off the extra leaves. Too many leaves would look messy. Everything should be perfect for Mrs. Bury today. It was her son the party was honoring, Timothy Bury. The youngest of her eight children. Timothy had just become a priest. Next fall session he would be teaching literature at the prestigious Ignatius High School.

Mrs. Bury had a lot of say-so about who taught what in that high school because she served as the most important lay member of the fundraising board. Her importance was well understood; her success on several other boards in the diocese where she had served for thirty years was also well understood; she never doubted her success, and no one was going to cheat her out of her place. Lela Bury was much accustomed to a place.

She came out of an old political family in the county that was well-to-do but not noted for anything especially, other than being able to win enormous government contracts. Which of course said it all for most people. For decades one relative or another of her family had been in the state legislature, or held judgeships, or served on the city council; they controlled literally thousands of patronage jobs, and owned land in some of the best places around — the airport and lake fronts, and out in the growing suburbs, so they were much respected for their wealth and kindness. And for their unkindness.

Yet what Lela Bury admired most of all were Jesuits, the Jesuit teachers, the strictness of the Jesuits. She admired them so much it was very likely she wanted to be one herself, but had to let it be enough that the honor was settled on her son. She had given a great deal to the order in terms of allotments and cash, and continued to do so, with most of her time now spent volunteering at the high school — a stunning building that looked like a small cathedral.

There she hid out in a modest dungeon-like office with her staff of other like- minded, dedicated mothers, smoking cigarettes and making endless phone calls to keep in touch with the lucrative alumni, whom she skillfully bullied for contributions. How good she was at it! How she separated them in a minute from their less important priorities and made them see where their real duties and obligations lay! It became a kind of penance to give to this well-known high school. And a defense of the faith. Didn't they know how Catholics were surrounded by enemies? Didn't they know how the old persecutors of the faith waited in the shadows for a time of weakness? Wasn't the press bringing up lies and smears against the holy fathers daily? You couldn't listen to a newscast without hearing some slander or another.

She knew what must be done to make them contribute. She wasn't afraid of their whining excuses. She knew all about them, even more than the priests themselves knew.

She pumped certain students, taking them right out of the halls and questioning them about their families.

Nothing was too small for her ears to know about. Did Mother and Father perhaps fight at night? Was this the reason for the poor grades? Were certain kids bringing stuff to school they shouldn't be bringing? Were certain classrooms becoming rowdy? A neighbor, herself with several sons, reported back to Lela recently what one of her sons had seen. "Oh, they have order at Ignatius," Mrs. Hurley told her. "None of that punky stuff going on there. When this one boy tried to wise off and couldn't learn — little wiseass who had no business in a good Catholic school like Ignatius in the first place. Well, Father Thomas had him stand up in front of the room and smacked him one, a good one right across the face. Then when he started and tears sprang in his eyes, Father made fun of him: 'Oh, what's the matter, did Father Thomas hurt your little feelings?' There were laughs and sneers from all the other boys. Then he slapped him again and forced him from the room."

Mrs. Bury and the tattling neighbor had laughed, for they knew the boy's mother. A little stuck-up convert who had no real respect for religion, who tried to argue with the fathers...tried to talk back to them on matters of faith! They had laughed in the kitchen with the dishwasher roaring over the pans and silverware. Well, everyone knew priests slapped boys. It was like a reward somehow. For the high tuition. You had to be tough with boys these days. Or the country would go on falling apart. Couldn't people see where all the laxness had got us, all the drugs and abortions?

Now the girl was polishing the last silver tray. Must be spotless and shiny. Wild goose, brother goose, which is best? She laid the forks and spoons out properly on the tables. Oh, the garbage can! It caught her eye...there was the rat poison box sticking up right in her face; she shoved it further down in the can and put on the lid, then carried the entire can down the steps to the cavernous sub-basement and hurried back up. This cheerless side-basement was where she had seen the rat, where she had laid down the poison, and an odor of wet decay clung to the air. The old stone floors of the mansion could use a good fumigating. She should lock the door just in case someone tried to go in there.

The first guests would be coming in right after the church bells sounded a second time across the park. She waited for the sound, standing in the kitchen, putting on her lipstick and combing out her hair. Her hair seemed dead, lifeless. She could use some new shampoo. A new brand. Her hair seemed to liven up when she changed brands. But she didn't want to use any of Mrs. Bury's — the very idea dug at something in her, because she saw that Mrs. Bury wanted her to use Mrs. Bury's things.

The older woman's generosity was oppressive this way. You were almost required to use her things — the way you were required to use her thoughts, think with her thoughts.

In a week or so Maylon would be stable enough to go back to work. She would find something. She didn't know what, exactly. Something. She had a suspended drug conviction against her in the courts.

Mrs. Bury — Lela — came into the room now, dressed in a bright pink suit with a flowered scarf folded to hide her baggy throat, yet looking like a fresh spasm of life, smelling powdered, and actually rejuvenated from a long, slow bath. She was a tall, bony-like woman of sixty, with a fluffy stand of reddish curly hair around her head. On the top of her head the hair was smooth and parted, then a little fluffy wreath of curls stood out, barely hiding the ears. She was putting on her earrings, and looking around at the tables, nodding. "That's good, Maylon. You've done a really great job. I knew you could if you tried. How does this look?" she pulled back her hair and exposed the earrings, flat round scarlet glass set in dark metal. Like traffic lights. Lela waited,her long face serious and suspenseful, expecting the girl to ask when she could borrow the earrings.

But Maylon did not answer. She did not know why. It came upon her not to respond. In this way, she was thinking, people jump off bridges. Just jump. "Well?" Lela demanded, her eyes widening and flashing with reproach. Still the girl did not answer, but only walked back to the tables, leaving the woman standing, holding her hair back from her ears.

Lela's face reddened in an angry, quick flush. It was the last thing she expected, being thwarted like this at the very moment everything was turning out so beautifully. She could hear herself reaching too quickly for an explanation, blurting and going out of control: "You want to spoil everything, don't you? It's your way of saying thank you for my having the judge send you here rather than to that louse-infested detention center, right?" As soon as she heard her own voice, raised in such hatred, she hated herself for it, but she had to go on, and more loudly than ever. She had to get it out. "Isn't that it? You want to throw it back in my face and cause a lot of bad feelings. And ruin everything. I know your kind. Stubborn and secretive, filling up with malice at the first chance you get! Well, you can forget about that, for I don't care what you think about my earrings. You hear that?"

"I know you don't care," the girl said sullenly over her shoulder, and Lela stood silent. She saw how ludicrously short the girl's skirt was then, right to the top of her skinny legs. Just covering her buttocks She wanted to object to this immodesty, but felt cornered. The girl would only buck her on this, and fluster the air even more with her stubborn face, just to make sure everybody had a good whiff of a quarrel in the air when they came in. Anything to be nasty! Anything to ruin someone's nice time. It was so unfair after all the work!

This woman was very proud of her involvement in the social rehabilitation of teen-aged girls. Especially the ones who had had abortions, the ones who had opened their flesh to lovers and then to doctors, who lay willingly in bed, and on tables, their bowels open to the bruising cold hands of men. It disgusted Lela. It was such trying work to make them see the value of self-respect.

But up until now this girl Maylon had shown such promise and remorse for her deviancy that Lela had been eager to show her off to the family today. Now she was wild with fault-finding at the very sight of her, this little piece of social merchandise she had taken into her home. They didn't want love; girls like this, they hated kindness. They were looking for thrills, the thrill of having their bodies turn to hot filth under some man. Who would then flush them out of sight in the sewer. She wanted to call Judge Wessly this instant and tell him to revoke the order. Because it wasn't working out. It would never work out. Because the girl had not praised her earrings. She removed her scarf and ran it carefully around her throat where she was so heated.

She was at a dangerous point now where she couldn't keep her heart from pounding, beating out of her chest with an almost-madness. She was half-smothering in her anger, knowing she was blind and not seeing straight. How could she be so stupid? She went into the kitchen, rushing, and took the sherry down from the pantry shelf with trembling, cold fingers. This would help; just the sweet, heavy shock of it in her mouth helped her come back to herself. Two good swallows and...there; two little swallows, there; she was comforted, caressed. There, one more swallow; and there, back down, back into sanity.

Yet her eyes flashed still with hatred. Just to know how satisfied the girl must be with herself! Smiling to herself, no doubt at forcing Lela to raise her voice like...what? It was unbearable. She felt she could actually kill this stubborn girl, although she didn't know why a person like that should drive her into such a state, a little ugly problem who thought she could sneer at the world and treat it like she treated her own body. She would send her away tonight, right after the garden party.

For further comfort she forced her mind onto her guests. Her family that was coming. She imagined them. Magnified them, their fresh faces and voices where she could bury her terrible disappointment as soon as they arrived. They would come in a troupe, with laughter and excitement radiating all around them. With such a family surrounding her, with such power in their excitement and happiness, no little mini-skirt off the street, some little thing who probably could never have any children, was going to hurt her, bring her almost to collapsing. Especially her Timothy. He would know how to set her straight! She better see that right now, better not start any pouting and nastiness in front of him. She felt she was going mad. Sweat broke out on her forehead. No, she was fine. Just fine. Another half-ounce of sherry would expand her arteries and let the blood through. Expand her veins. Then she could think straighter. It was best to stay a little drunk in this miserable world.

In time, the tall doors of the old brick-and-stone mansion were flung open upon the spring sunlight and people began coming in. They looked strikingly the same, all good, Irish-looking faces, some of them handsome and lovely , but all confident and proud and knowing, Lela thought to herself. As good Catholics they had seized upon the perfect rhythm of life — the promise of their special spiritual heritage, rational and poignant, and incomprehensible, of course, but passing on to them out of Lela Bury and her strong-willed kind, so they would hold on to it, with no listening to the wrong voices, no turning aside from the learned routines of their own teachings. None of that barren radicalism you heard coming from certain quarters out of the new, expanding university across town. This was the way the world should be, with everyone dressed up in bright church clothes, getting ready to eat a nice buffet, stuffing in food and cracking jokes and teasing one another. They all had wonderful jobs. Even the women were making money, laying up their own enormous fortunes.

Timothy Bury came for the first time in his priest's garb.

He stood on the wide porch with its newly-washed red tiles, his arms thrown open to his mother, who was coming down the entrance hall, tall and steady in good, medium-sized heels. He puckered his lips and gave her a loud warm kiss, smelling the scent of sherry on her breath as he did. It was a scent he smelled more and more often since his father's death two years ago, and something gave way inside him, almost to brimming his eyes. Thank the saints for her fine volunteer work with troubled teen-aged girls; she was a credit to the faith this way just as her fundraising was a credit to the parish. She was quite the success in his eyes; nevertheless, something pulled at him, and he couldn't help worrying.

His large blue eyes took in the room. There was a strange pallor to his skin now, as if it were part of his dress, a holy ascetic pallor to go with his black frock. He was tall and lanky like his mother, with brownish, clean hair and fresh skin, and an unfaltering priestly smile, as if something very significant were about to happen, something superstitious, sensational, even frightening — but all of it calmly accepted, even calmly welcomed and perfectly understood by his prayer-braced mind.

Maylon came into the room to help take the coats, and he stared at her briefly. He knew about her. He had read her record with Judge Wessley, with his mother looking on. They were confident she would benefit from Lela Bury. Lela would straighten her out, although Timothy believed it would be better if the girl did some time at the reformatory. With a little suffering, a little humiliation, she would better appreciate what was being done for her. His eyes went back to the girl as if she were the only interest that concerned him. As if he had kept her on his mind all day.

Then suddenly it happened. Suddenly he was aware of something, like a flash in his head; he was taken aback by a strong shock. It took him several seconds to comprehend it, but when this girl in her short skirt bent forward with her back to him, he saw everything she had. That is, she was not wearing a stitch of underclothes. No panties. Her bottom was as bare as a rubber doll's. He quickly looked away, and into the faces of the others around the room. Had they noticed as well? No. No one else apparently had encountered this daft vision of the young bare ass, with its little shadow of a crack that ran up between the soft mounds of flesh, like a groove in a peach. He looked at his mother now, who shook her head for him not to say anything. And he did as she directed, his face glowing warm with embarrassment.

Maylon went around with a tray of toys, small nonsense toys to keep the younger children amused: little cars and Chinese handcuffs, small jars for blowing soap bubbles. She was offering the various pieces to the children. Letting them choose. Yet she seemed alone, a sort of stray, all but forgotten in the brisk chatter of the house. Just let her bend over like that once more. Just let her dare!

When he worked his way back to the kitchen, his mother drew him into the pantry and emptied her thoughts against the girl. She had to go. She was impossible. Couldn't be trusted. She had not responded to decent kindness. So let her learn. "Why, she doesn't have on a stitch of...she's not dressed, Mother, I hope you've noticed." His mother thought he meant only the short skirt. She didn't know about the girl deliberately exposing herself to Timothy, as he believed she had. It was all beyond normal belief. What could the girl be thinking? She must be crazier than he or his mother realized. A person like that might do anything.

But Timothy could only speak in platitudes. "I'm praying this moment to the blessed saints for help, Mother. But look, you've helped so many others. Ah, listen, Mother — don't cry. We won't let the devil take this day meant for our happiness. What exactly has she done to you?"

He thought again of the girl's rear-end. It had looked so pale and lurid, utterly contemptible. But his mind jumped to the fact that women all over the country were exposing themselves in front of the news cameras. Showing contempt for the body was a growing fad. Look at what they did in New Orleans last Mardi Gras. Tattoos and body piercings. Slicing the skin, making mutilations and God knew what savage thing would come next. The Church always had its job cut out for it; that was one sure thing.

"Turning up their rumps right to the cameras." Someone said this in the garden. So they too were talking about the Mardi Gras now. But why now? Why? Someone else must have seen the girl bend over, of course.

"Oh, the cameras deserve it," his uncle Seamus declared. Seamus was a vigorous-looking man in his sixties, a brother to Lela, who came trotting up with a little girl riding his shoulders. He too had been a teacher, but now he sat in the Common Council and he had seen his share. "And don't think you priests are left out of everything, Timothy, ha ha. Look at your Merton. That Thomas Merton of the Seven Story Mountain. He had his fill. Went out to California. Smoked weed. Got laid. Ran around with Reds and Atheists."

"The only thing I remember about that book," Timothy said, finding himself quivering, raising his hands in helpless irony after what he had seen, "is the rabbit chase. Yes, here they are in a car. In Italy, I believe. Car loaded with people, racing downhill, can't stop, they are flying, and this jackrabbit is in front of the headlights. Hopping in front of the head beams. The road is so narrow. A cliff on one side, the sea on the other, and the mad rabbit won't get out of the road, but keeps ahead of the car. Flying and hopping. That's about all I remember."

"I remember how he died.' It was Maylon who spoke now, in a very quiet voice, almost crouching forward as if she had come out of the walls.

"And how's that, honey?" Seamus said, turning his head slightly to her. "I forget. Some kind of accident, wasn't it?" His head was bent down while the child pulled at his ears.

"Electrocution," Maylon said quickly. It was very strange how she said it. As if electrocution were a wonderful choice made by a man who knew what he was doing. Timothy could feel her consciously at work now, her need to exert and reveal herself to Seamus. Obviously she gravitated to men, needing men, wanting an older lover to save her. Young girls, he knew from hearing confessions, liked to have sex with older men, although Seamus would claim it was news to him.

"My friend Mike loved that man. And the wonderful letters he wrote to Flannery," she volunteered further.

"Oh, yeah, Flannery O'Connor, you mean? Our little Dixie Catholic. You going to teach Flannery's stories, Timothy?" Seamus asked, trotting the little girl around in a circle.

Timothy was putting a piece of candy in his mouth. A piece of chocolate he had picked up from the tray no one else was finding. He turned a second ball of chocolate around in his fingers and chewed, shaking his head to show he couldn't speak for a second.

"I hoped you would. Flannery wrote a lot about female entrapment, you know. Young adult females entrapped at home by impossible parents of one kind or another. I interpret this as meaning the struggling mind itself entrapped within an old abusive Christian ethic."

"Oh, do you really?" Timothy said. He did not know who Flannery O'Connor was.

"We visited her home in Georgia." Maylon said, holding the silver tray against her hip and wrinkling her forehead. This was a subject that obviously meant something to her. "Mike had to see her house. He was my boyfriend. Mike Falzone. That was a few years ago. I forget exactly which year, but we were just teenagers. Fourteen and eighteen. Mike and me. On his bike. He was a biker. We went all the way to Milledgeville, Georgia on it just to see her house, but no one there in town even knew who she was. Finally we saw this big, white, gothic-looking house. That's not it, I said. That is too much like how it should be, how I would imagine it to be. It was in the college area. Students and faculty were living in the big houses around it. But this one house was falling into ruin. The roof was sagging off."

"I can't really believe that," Timothy said, swallowing the last taste of chocolate.

"But it's true. We took pictures. I still have them. The house and lawns took up half the block. The back part was walled-in with a big, fine, ivy-covered wall. Just like this one we're standing in. That's where her peacocks walked. So Mike yelled out to some guy walking by. Some guy in a suit of clothes. 'Where's that O'Connor house?' he yelled. The guy didn't even look at us, just threw out his arm and pointed like he was tired of people asking. Over there, he pointed to the house. So that was it. I was awe-struck. I got off the bike and walked around. There was a chain across the wide steps. And a sign that read *Private Home*. It was all rotting and sad-looking. We both had tears in our eyes. From the other side I saw someone was in there. Just standing by the back kitchen door, looking out. A woman with a cup in her hand, standing under a bare light. I said, 'I bet that's her mother.' And later on I was told that her mother was actually still living there. So it must have been her, Regina."

"Regina?" Timothy scoffed, "Regina?"

"Yes, Flannery's mother. Regina," the girl said, not looking at him. "They're famous."

"If they're so famous, why was their house falling down to the ground?"

"Well, we didn't know. But we went to complain. To the Chamber of Commerce. To the little college, too.

And they said they couldn't do anything. 'We don't own the O'Connor property,'.It was all very puzzling. I don't know if they fixed the house or what. But it's been a long time."

"Well, on second thought, Flannery O'Connor might be falling out of fashion," Seamus went on. "Not enough raw sex in her stuff. Today no matter what an industry tries to market, it ends up marketing sex. Have you noticed? Whether it's music or books, or poetry, it all comes back to sex. Look at who does the news. So I ask you, who needs a sex maniac to deliver your news, I ask you that? To tell you who's bombing the Serbs? So they've got this gorgeous out-front chick reporting. Just so people can look at her and say to themselves *this, this is the kind of company I deserve. This is who I need to sit with at the breakfast table in the morning*, those long, smooth legs crossed, whispering, 'Now, Bob, this morning a ten-year-old stole a car and then hopped a plane…' But now, if you had some fat ugly black Sambo telling it..."

"Well, I've seen some real niggers moving the news, let me tell you. I mean some big, fat black mothers," another man said, a young man who was laughing and flushed red in the face.

"Hey, Keith, I don't wanna hear that. You shouldn't talk like that! Are you drunk already? I thought you were going to leave that stuff alone today."

"No, I'm not drunk!" Keith said, straightening with pretended outrage.

"It's like this," Seamus said, "today people act like sex is something you've got to have. *Got* to, I mean. Or you DIE! Like it's water."

"Yeah, give me a cool glass of sex before I die, ha ha." Keith's flushed face roared loudly.

"Seamus was laughing as well. He was having a good time. The little girl was pulling his ears out from his head and making a snorting noise. "And have you noticed the book jackets lately? Even on the mechanical drawing books the authors look like pin-ups. Or like...like hunks... big, eager Sex Gods. Even the editors have to pose. It's too much for the normal mind. I think it's because all sex in America is vicarious. I really think no one wants sex. They just want to talk about it, think about it. Keep it at a distance. They are always thinking about it. Looking at a murder trial, they see themselves in bed with the murderer. Or the good-looking lawyer. But do they do it? Not likely. I would write a book about it, but the subject is too beneath me."

"If it's so vicarious, why all the abortions?" Timothy asked. He refused to see the humor in such a wayward subject. He glanced at the girl, hoping to shame her. Obviously she felt she was getting somewhere with Seamus. Pretending she knew so much. But she would not be put down; she stared back at him boldly, close to his face until it was he who turned away, feeling soiled and confronted.

He walked away among the tables crowded with cousins and wives chatting and laughing. On one of the tables was a bowl of chocolates. Timothy picked up two pieces and nibbled them greedily. He had been fasting, starving himself. He took two more pieces. He moved aside as the girl came out and put some more pieces of chocolates into the bowl and then went back to the kitchen. This disturbed him for some reason, as if his heart were clinging close and tight while some danger went near it.

She returned calmly with a huge silver coffee server, a piece that had been in the family for eighty years. He watched her skinny arm tremble under its weight as she poured into the cups. He was thinking about what Seamus had said...the stupid obsessions people had with sex. He had not known the full extent of this secret, muffled thinking in people until he had been sent into the hospitals to hear confessions. Especially the women. Even old women. The old laid-up skeletons told him fantastic tales, all made-up with care, their eyes blinded with pleasure. "Oh, Father, Father I have sinned. I was one of the white women who took drugs and partied around the country with — you'll never guess — Martin Luther King! Yes, I was a favorite of his. Hell will be worth the price, I tell you...Father, don't hate me for this..." It was amazing how so many of them wanted in their dreams to be the lovers of dark men. "Hell will be worth the price, Father! And I am with child this minute, although I am ninety-two years old. I am going to have a baby in the spring."

He could hear Seamus still talking as he trotted another little girl under the budding tree branches. "Sometimes I think everything...I mean, everything...is made-up. Don't people really live anymore? They let the television crank their brains. They've lost their minds to ad men."

The girl was still nearby, carrying coffee on a tray. His eyes followed her once more as she bent from the waist and he narrowed them painfully, trying to see. Had he actually been wrong? This time he could not see her bare skin, for she was now wearing very light pantyhose, very sheer with a sheen of pearl.

His mother must have made her go upstairs and slip them on. The girl's feet were very small and narrow in leather loafers. Her legs very slender and child-like. She was watching him. Looking over at him.

He was suddenly aware of a discomfort in his stomach. The chocolate felt suddenly heavy. He didn't want to eat anymore. It seemed to burn his stomach. The girl looked around at him...why? Why was she staring — to see if he was getting sick? He glanced around for someplace to put the extra piece of chocolate. It was melting on his fingers. Where were the trash cans? His mother always kept a nice new one out at the garden parties. And shouldn't he get a plastic bag and help pick up the paper plates and cups?

"Let me," Jonathan was saying, taking the bag out of Timothy's hands. Jonathan was a close friend and, like Timothy, the young man would become a priest. He was living now at Sacred Heart Noviciate. They had come here together. Timothy made a motion to his stomach. "Don't eat any of that stuff she's put out in that bowl," he said, making a sour face.

"Not agreeing with you, Father?"

"Not at all. I think I want a glass of water." He drank a glass of cold water, alarmed by his thirst. The water made him feel strange, dizzy.

"Where has the new garbage can gone?" his mother said.

Maylon pointed down to the sub-basement. When Jonathan emerged back on the steps, he said, "Door's locked."

"Why are the doors locked?" Lela asked; she knew when anything was out of order.

"I don't know," the girl said. Timothy was looking at her as she reached for the key. She knew exactly where the key was. Because she had used it last. Why did she lie? Why did his mother trust her with keys?

Now they were down the basement stairs with Timothy holding himself coldly at a small distance. Now was his chance to tell her while she held the lock and inserted the key with such a deft, criminal hand. "You better keep away from the men upstairs," he told her frankly. "They want nothing to do with you. You're about to make a little nuisance of yourself."

The girl did not answer. She went back up the steps. Timothy pushed the door open and nearly fell into the dark. A slice of evening sunlight fell across his back, onto the concrete floor. And there he saw the dead rat, stiff, its paws curled as if in a painful dream. The rotting smell of it, heavy and damp, rushed into his face. Then he saw the empty box of rat poison. He closed the door and retreated. The foul scent made him want to vomit. And he was so thirsty! For the rest of the afternoon he was aware of it, a horrible thirst which the water couldn't touch. There wasn't water cold enough to get at it. He wanted to drink water that was on the very edge of freezing. He wanted a whole pitcher of it with crushed, icy pieces whirling into his stomach.

His stomach was beginning to ache, as if a slow acrid glue lay in its pit. In his agitation he wondered how long everyone was going to stay. And how long it might take him to die. He had to be leaving. It had grown dark outside. The street lights had come on, but the children were still laughing in the garden. His mother was bringing a birthday cake out with candles throwing up little black smoke trails. They were singing to his aunt Virginia who had just turned fifty. Fifty! But he couldn't be bothered with Virginia's fifty years when his own life might end at any moment in death. He was very ill, but he could not bring himself to tell anyone. He had always been that way. Into himself. Keeping things to himself. Now he would die without telling anyone.

"Jonathan," he said, "I'm about ready. I think it is time we said our leave."

He conferred with his mother. She must not be soft about getting rid of the girl. She must stick to their agreement. No matter what. It annoyed him that his mother had taken on a better mood, and seemed ready to have another try with the girl. "You'll regret that," he told her. His face was ashen and damp. His mother stared at him. He seemed so unhappy for some reason. "My stomach is bothering me," he said, brushing it all away. He was ready to die.

But once in the car with Jonathan driving, he was so ill he had to explain what was happening to him. It was all right to tell Jonathan. "Jonathan, I'm very sick. Sicker than you would want to know. But I think you should understand that something is very wrong. I have been poisoned. Deliberately so, I believe. It was that chocolate. That girl staying with Mother. She's poisoned me. I'm certain of it."

The young man looked at him. "If you're sick, we better go to a doctor. To the emergency room."

"Pull over here!" Timothy yelled in desperation, reaching for the door handle and throwing himself halfway out the door as it pulled into the park. He vomited profusely, the sweat breaking out on his body and his limbs trembling in fear. He was making a frightful noise, very embarrassing to Jonathan, who was afraid the police might come around and shine a light in his face. Accuse him of something.

"Are you better now? Do you feel some better?" he asked hopefully. He could see how pale Father Timothy was; his head lay back, corpse-white. Jonathan began to tremble himself. Yet he couldn't believe the priest had really been poisoned. "Just put your face out the window, keep it in the air. You'll be fine. Crowds do that to me too sometimes. Make me sick. All the talking you have to do and everything. Are you sure you're better?" He could see that he was. He could see how soft and even Timothy's breathing was, and he drove on, towards the noviciate, his face distorted with disgust.

Blindness

OUR REGION OF THE SOUTHERN APPALACHIANS LIES DIRECTLY IN the path of migrating birds whose droppings carry the hateful tracomatis, a contagious bacteria that causes a disease of the eyes known to result in blindness if not treated.

In the late '40s there was an outbreak of this disease among the school children where we lived in a little isolated trainstop of a place. No one knew what to call it at first; we just knew that when a person became infected his red and watery eyes looked weak, as if he had been crying. Like he had been slapped. Some of the kids started calling it the whipped pup disease, and even after we learned its real name, a few continued to call it this.

So luckily the patients had to leave home to be treated, out of sight of his classmates, who were as good as you can find anywhere when it came to tormenting others with something wrong with them.

He would need to go to Richmond where there was a fine clinic with specialists, and where there was also the famous Welner House, a guest home operated by Miss Geneva Welner, who took in poor country children and their parents free of charge while being treated in town for eye complaints.

So when this new outbreak occurred, several families descended upon Welner House at the same time, a dozen or so small patients. They rode in a taxi from the train depot, down the hazy brick streets to where the fanciful old stone mansion sat silent as a cliff, jutting out of the tall cedars and dogwoods that surrounded it on all sides.

Guests came timidly up to the enormous shiny doors, glancing around as if mystified that someone who owned such a place could be interested in their little red-eyed malady. The tall doors supported an old-fashioned, heavy brass knocker, and when you reached up for it, you naturally looked higher and saw yourself in a bright hanging globe projection of some sort in the ceiling, a fixture clutched in the curly metal claws of a lion's paw. The globe was very ornate and covered in a thin metallic paint that made a shiny mirror in which you looked back at yourself so distorted you gasped out loud for a second, then you couldn't resist posturing and twisting to see what other freakish faces you could arrange before the door was pulled opened.

However, every one of these visitors, no matter what mood the silly mirror put them in, carried the terrible fear of blindness with them, just as they carried their pathetic little beaten-up suitcases and cardboard boxes and paper sacks with their belongings. This fear was very distressing to the nerves, and they looked forward to some kindness that might match these lofty walls and manicured lawns.

But once the large doors were opened, nothing they saw relaxed their anxieties. The rooms were very dark and strange-looking with people all over the place trying to find out what to do next, but there was not a friendly face anywhere.

It just so happened then, that on this day of rushing and pushing, a hefty woman, grinning broadly and obviously blind as a discarded light bulb, crept stealthily from somewhere, through the crowd, and into the center of the room, gleefully determined to take advantage of the chaos. Before anyone could stop her she clapped her hands to get attention and began to make a threatening speech to the newcomers, touching on all the fears they were trying to hide. "A-ha, so the birds are still going ka-ka over the woods and rivers of the north fork district, huh?" she cried loudly. "And flushing out another crowd of little diseased puppies into the hands of the almighty doctors. They'll do for you what they've done for me! Just look!" She threw back her head and howled as if overjoyed with the notion. "Look at my eyes! You think they can't see, but I see everything!" She rolled her sightless eyes around which looked to everyone, as they agreed later in whispers, exactly like two spots of pigeon droppings.

The guests stood in bewilderment while the woman roared on with her fleshy, gap-toothed mouth growing more and more violent, until by degrees they glanced at one another in near panic. "Nobody's going to do anything for you here except experiment on you, I can tell you that much! And when they've finished their nasty experiments, you'll be marched down into the basement and drowned in the wash tubs like little kittens, your heads held under the water long as you move!" She shouted with the jeering, nervous laugh that never left her thick lips. But now, for just five dollars, I'll lay my hands on your eyes and those eyes will be free from all the diseases of blindness. Trust me, I tell you!"

"Hey, shoo! Shoo! Shut your mouf, ol' mean woman Gracie Washburn! Now, shut it — you hear me talkin' to you!" Gracie was suddenly being pulled away and scolded by a voice louder than her own that startled her into silence. "Now, look at chew! Haint chew ashamed of yourself now?"

This second woman was a tall, slender, warm-skinned black woman. She had grabbed Gracie's arm and was shaking her fleshly round contours with a furious motion.

"Miss Geneva, she say she don't want you, mean Gracie lady, in this house for another night the way you been acting and carrying on. And I don't blame her one little bit. Three days of the likes of you is enough for anybody, let alone people busy like we is. The ways yous go around lying on eberbady you can. Saying how yous can cure blind peoples. Why that's a sin, and yous know it's a sin."

"Leave me be if you don't want me to get even. 'Cause you know I can. You know I can cure the blind! That's what you're afraid of. You know I can do the cure on blind people."

"Why don't you cure yourself?"

"It's not meant to be. But I see beyond."

"I see."

"Now turn loose! I'll get even with you all, you wait and see if I don't. I know a few things," Gracie shouted again, pulling away and panting with anger, her eyes rolling wildly. The black woman glared, not to be intimidated, her face unafraid. She had awakened the confidence of the room with her manner and her dainty, starched appearance, her white lace apron and long grey dress and white polished shoes.

"Oh, please, please, pay no attention to all this noise!" another voice now rang out, addressing the room. "Gracie was just leaving," she said in a busy way, "Better show her into the garden and let her collect herself."

This third woman was Miss Geneva Welner, calm and melodious, who had come into the room, followed by two assistants with clipboards on which they were taking notes in Braille.

Everyone knew about Miss Geneva. They had heard her talked about all over the country, her secrets turned into a public chew rag. Now they were looking at her for the first time. A near legend. But she gave off no excitement, a very plain, thin woman, beginning to age. Perhaps with a slightly vaunted air they had seen in missionary women, the unmarried ones who came around testifying and baptizing people in the rivers. Living for a summer in the cramped settlement houses and then disappearing back to who knew where.

The garden Geneva referred to as within the confines of a stone wall out back, where there were also an old carriage house and stable that had once connected the grounds to a back area of weedy meadow and orchards, but now opened with a barred gate to the foggy parking lots of the hospital.

Several people in work clothes rose to let Gracie sit at the green ornate iron table under the trees. She began to toss pebbles at the crowing roosters and peacocks that had the range of the grounds. From time to time her laughing voice floated back into the room where Geneva stood in her long-coated suit of some colorless silky material, with her light chestnut hair done up in a careful way in a crescent roll just off her neck with not a strand loose anywhere. And there was the brooch of gold and pearl fastened at her throat.

The brooch was famous. Everyone had heard about it. How it had been given to her by Dr. Leonard Todd, whose full-sized oil portrait now hung in the entrance hall of the house. Geneva had been engaged to him at his death. He had been killed in the war a month before the wedding. Dr. Todd had been an eye surgeon. Geneva was never without the brooch.

People said to watch and you would see her fingers reach for it absently as she talked. And so she did. The long cool pale fingers went in a seeking way, toying with the brooch as she explained everything, all the rules of the house, where each person would sleep, where the meals would be served, and how to report to the clinic which lay out back beyond the garden and parking lots.

Everyone was still thinking about the miserable Gracie Washburn claiming to cure the blind, and wondering if they had not heard her name before. They thought about her. Tried to place her. Obviously she was trash. They stopped thinking about her as they strolled around silently looking at the portraits of the eye surgeon, a strikingly handsome man, like a movie star, a shock after meeting Miss Geneva, who seemed half a mystery of ugliness in comparison with her unbloomed womanhood and proud nose and hard Scots jaw. "How on earth could a doctor as handsome as Leonard Todd be in love with Geneva Welner, someone about as warm as a frog gigging pole?" the other women asked in whispers once they were off to themselves.

It was a subject much turned over in the dark in their rooms, just as it had at one time taken up most of the conversation in the country. It was now almost impossible to connect the two faces, one so handsome, dead seven years, since 1942. And the other a glut of nostalgia that entangled the whole town.

The wedding should have been a June one. With mountains of flowers and an enormous reception on the lawns of the Todd estate, with Chinese lanterns shining in the trees and little boats strung out on the river carrying candles and umbrellas.

Some people still kept their invitations, just to have something to mention when they showed their scrap books. It was said that several seamstresses worked in shifts on the gowns, fitting and refitting the wedding dress as Geneva lost weight from the excitement.

"This will kill her for sure," the older women said about the doctor's death. They wanted a nervous breakdown to talk about, or so Geneva's mother observed.

"He's the only thing she's ever had, so you know it's going to kill her. She always did remind me of one of these mousy types who put on like they're in such perfect control, but then you discover they're swallowing down all kinds of pills just to keep their heads from blowing off."

"Well, if they want to see a nervous breakdown they can go over to the asylum and see one," Geneva's mother sent word to that effect, "for it's not going to be Geneva's they see."

And off they flew to New Orleans where there were relatives and where Geneva could let her poor heart heal in that Garden of Eden with its misty landscape of fountains and enclosing atmosphere of dreaming, sleepwalking crowds milling forever in the lush palm, waving squares.

"Oh, she's a fine one, all right," they said. "What does she think she's going to find down in ahleans?"

"I hear you don't find anything in ahleans. You lose it."

"She'll end up with a nigger, that's what. You mark my words," Betty Moss, the hairdresser said out-loud. "Bet you five dollars."

This was still the old segregated South, where if a woman traveled away from her hometown she was going off to find a black man to raise the level of excitement in her life. For what else could she be looking for? And the same was true of any strange woman coming into the community to live. She must be running away from some black man she had been laying around with up in New York or Detroit.

"Oh, now you girls ought not to talk like that. Shame on you," the better women chided. They were above such talk themselves, but still they expected to hear it. It did them good to know the lower whites, lower than themselves certainly, felt the dangers of the black population around them, as if they, the higher-ups, were expected to do something about it. It had a flattering warm effect. They could float in this crude intimate talk while their hair was being dressed, lifted and fingered and lovingly attached to weird machines that resembled the electric chair in a death chamber. They liked to hear it, just as they liked to hear how Dr. Todd could have done better courting one of their daughters rather than that poor little ol' turkey-footed Geneva Welner.

But Geneva went her own way. She flowed away in another direction, inside the half-invisible world of ophthalmic medicine where Dr. Todd had been so well admired, and where these friends saw that Welner House received its share of funding, support, and full recommendations of the clinical staff.

Perhaps she was a bit too driven at times, in a kind of imprisonment, in which her bird-like energy never stopped for breath, never got close to anyone, but never missed a thing out of place.

Like this Gracie Washburn business. The woman was revolting with her hairy arms and fat neck. She fought with everyone and simply had to be driven off. When Gracie offered to pay twice as much to live at Welner's as required, Geneva had snapped back, "Money is not the problem here. It isn't the answer, either. *I'm* the answer. What I say goes. And I say you go. I'm not running an orphanage or a flophouse."

A low curse rose in Gracie's throat, so distinct and ugly that Geneva was to remember it even years later with a shiver.

"You'll fall apart one day, I predict it! You'll go blind too!" she panted. "And then I'll be even."

They were again escorting Gracie, but she had stopped her screaming and was grinning to herself.

"She can make her way home by feeling along the fences...if not, someone will act as a guide. Just check and see that she doesn't leave anything around here to come back for," Geneva ordered, and ascended the stairs with her head lowered in reflection over this trifling circumstance. "Get even with me?" she scoffed. "What can a thing like you with your big ass do to get even with me?"

Part II

The contagions subsided. Five busy years passed. When Geneva was thirty-five her mother died while drinking out of a bottle she kept hidden in a fake Bible.

Geneva went through a period of being lost, as if walking in a dark wind. Her eyes protruded as if straining to make out the way, but they didn't have to strain long. For the old lady, it was later learned, had left her daughter a fortune. Even Geneva was amazed at the amount and gathered herself up, ready to do battle. She had clout now, as they say. She really began to understand people for the first time, a very simple matter, just as her mother had said. It did not take long for everyone to realize that if you wanted to raise money in that town for your charity or cause, you'd better not be on the wrong side of Miss Geneva Welner, for reasons you might soon understand.

When another two years had slipped away the governor himself came to town and gave her an award for her work with the blind. She now lived well out of reach of the nasty claws of the poor and beyond the hammer of the rich. She was a fine lady of the town, and after a while it actually became impossible not to praise the woman, as if just seeing her on the street was enough to cause people to jump up from their chairs and say something extraordinary about her character, simply because everyone else did. "*Oh, there she goes, she never spares herself!*" or "*I'd do anything for that woman*"; "*She's as good as a moral gets on this earth*"; "*The town is lucky to have her to brag about, I'll tell you!*" and so forth.

This adulation became a habit and the habit became something almost brainless, and to prove it, there was a ballad written about her and the heroic doctor who had died on the battlefields of France, so beyond the bounds of good taste that Geneva herself requested the thing be crushed and never again played in her presence. In a small town, a public figure can take just so much praise before striking back.

PART III

However there was one major item about her life that drew no attention. It was amazing, most of all precisely because to the people around her, it did not seem to merit attention. And that was this: although Geneva was now forty years old, and although she had suddenly taken on a special radiance and thrust of vigor that seemed to glow from down under her fine, clear flesh and make it look like deep, cool, untouched Vaseline, there was no man for her.

No one mentioned this. It was as if a subconscious, dogged modesty or shame had set in, the way an instinct against incest is said to do, that prevented even a discussion of the fact that no man aside from Dr. Leonard Todd had ever found her attractive.

Perhaps it was enough to think of the handsome doctor, hanging so young and marvelous on the wall under the light as the only love she would ever need to know — or as her old mother said before she died, "How many women can get a doctor to touch them even when they're sick, let alone get engaged to one?" So there was no need to feel sorry for Geneva.

It was a little annoying, offensive even, to think of her as needing someone else. There she was with her public tragic virginity, sitting like some kind of shrine behind her high wall of money, coming and going through the town in her big carful of kids.

And what about that army of old clinic people she knew, admirers of her doctor? Always jumbled up at the country club dinners, nodding their heads about their golf scores and stock market reports. That was enough for her. Anything deeper should not cross a normal person's mind.

So for a long time everyone just went on living in a smooth resolute propriety, which was well enough until Geneva involved herself in an event that not only compelled them to think about her, but actually demanded their alarmed attention.

Everyone asked the same question: how could such a settled, safe and significant life such as Geneva Welner's take the fantastic divergent path it now took? The answer was beyond all their imaginations laid end to end.

Part IV

The event began late one night around the beginning of the holidays, on one clear night in December with the church bells ringing the usual carols over the cold, decorated streets. Welner House, which usually held half a dozen guests, as a rule, was now empty except for the three live-in servants. The rooms had been freshly turned out and cleaned. Cakes were baked for an open house tea to be held the following afternoon. A lighted Christmas tree stood in the large front window, casually blinking its spiked image against the tall, polished squares of glass.

Geneva was in her private quarters on the second floor, clipping out an article from the local newspaper. She expected no visitors this time of evening. But out of the corner of her eye she noticed the shining beams of a car's headlights turning slowing into the alleyway that was used for deliveries to the back entrance.

The lights disappeared. Miss Geneva listened and stood up. A car door slammed in the dark; there was a shuffle of heavy boots on the cold bricks, then a loud knocking against the back door pounded in the silence. She heard the feet of the servant girl, then the locks being thrown. There were three locks on the door which then was stopped by a chain.

"Who you?" Mildred Esther, the number-one cook asked, putting her mouth up to the crack in the chained door and watching her breath curl out on the cold air. "This ain't no door for no night company. This here door's exclusive for the daytime mans doin' deliveries. What you want?"

"It's me, Easy White, from over at the race tracks. Mr. Connell — he sent me to talk to Miss Geneva about somethin' right now. I'm riding his car tonight and I'm in a hurry to get it back to him."

"Miss Geneva don't come to no back door. And she don't have no business with your likes, walking nor a-riding."

"You go get her like I tell you and stop actin' around or I'll be in there and cut your head clean off your shoulders, girl. Now, go. I got real business, understand that."

"Gonna go tell her what you say, fool," Mildred Esther said slowly as she turned and went up to fetch Miss Geneva.

"He's down there handling the worst kind of talk there is. He say not to come back without you. Say Mr. Connell sent him in his car and he wants to cut me if I don't bring you."

"Cut you! We'll see who gets cut. Tell him to stand right where he is. We'll see about pulling a knife around my place here," Geneva said, angrily snatching a robe and marching down the stairs and back through to the kitchen.

"Worse talk you ever heard," Mildred Esther continued, following behind Geneva who went past the back door where the caller stood waiting on the other side and down on to the basement stairs where she yelled, "Andy! I need you up here right now and bring your thirty-eight and load it. I'm not going to let people think they can start demanding from me if I can help it. I don't owe this Connell anything," she shouted, pulling open the door now into the rough face of a tall black man. He was holding a baby in his arms.

It was a moment of intense astonishment, so unexpected was the sight of the strong black arms embracing the small wrapped bundle. The baby began to scream, helplessly, as if in pain. It was a very light-skinned black child, with well-formed legs that kicked, and well-formed arms that flayed the air as it filled the room with its horrendous wailings.

Stunned, Geneva automatically reached for the child and took it in her arms as if something compelled her. It was a boy; they could tell from its muscular size. She moved away with him rapidly, into the light. She seemed to know something that frightened her. "He's blind. He's blind, isn't he?" she said. The black man at the door did not answer. "Yes. He's blind." she said emphatically now. "It's his eyes that are making him scream like this. They hurt him. It's syphilis, I'm sure."

"The ol' syph!" Mildred Esther screeched with a horror of repugnance. She talked without turning to the man, her face in another direction. "Yo' all come in here with the ol' debil's doings, fool! I knowed yo' all weren't no good!" She lifted the hem of her skirt up over her nose and mouth to protect herself while going into a moaning humming sound, half-prayer, half-incantation of terror. "That the way he do you. Lawdy, the ol' debil he do you like this. Come right in your back door in the winter time. Lawdy, have mercy on us all in here tonight!"

"Shut up with that Lawdy stuff," Geneva said to Mildred Esther, then to another woman, "Caroline, call the hospital. Call them now! And tell them we are on our way over with an emergency case. Tell them Miss Geneva said to get Dr. Floyd there to attend a special case. Tell them I want the eye clinic specialists called into an emergency conference."

"And you," she said to the Easy White at the door, "If you don't want to go back to the state prison where Mr. Connell got you from, you better not show your face around here sassing my women like they were some of those things you and Mr. Connell associate with."

"Yes'um," the man said, withdrawing. "But this ain't none of my fault."

When the servant attempted to take the baby from Geneva, she moved out of her reach. "I'll hold him," she said firmly. "You go get the car and start it up. Let it warm up good. Real good and warm. Shuush," she spoke to the child who wailed relentlessly.

For days he continued to cry without letting up. The hospital could do nothing. The pain was like nothing they had seen before, disturbing in the extreme to all who witnessed it. Geneva remained with the tormented infant, holding him in her arms with a look of motherly distress on her long pale cheeks.

At the end of the week, Dr. Floyd came to her with a diagnosis. It was as Geneva had feared. The child had been infected since before birth. He was sightless, but otherwise pronounced sound. Then he told her what she already knew: the eyes would have to be removed or the pain would either kill the patient or stunt his mind forever. There was no time to sit and consider. The eyes were removed the next morning in a long operation.

Geneva cancelled all her appointments and stayed at the hospital the whole time. She held the baby in her arms constantly, unaware of her own exhaustion in every limb. No one could feed him but Geneva. He was her baby now. And although the town was drop-mouthed at the news, she decided to take him home after he recovered and began legal adoption proceedings. She named him Leonard. Linnie, for short.

The nursery at Welner House had several infant cribs, but these were removed and only one new crib, specially made for Linnie, was allowed to remain. There were boxes of musical toys, and large stuffed animals and a bed for Geneva. She wanted to sleep close to the child in case he needed her. And he needed her constantly. He was amazingly hungry and eager for food now that his body was free of pain.

Geneva loved to carry his strong, chubby little body against her shoulder and stand in front of the windows with him and gaze dreamily out at nothing but the town and trees.

As he grew she liked to ride him around on her hip, cuddling and cooing to him non-stop. He was very active, strong and willful. He liked to throw objects out of his crib and listen to them with delight as they crashed against the floor and walls. "That won't do, Mildred Esther scolded in protest. Who you think is going to clean up all that mess? To my mind he goin' to have to learn who he is one of these days, that's all."

Geneva heard this last remark and went silent in thought for the next two days. It struck her that Mildred Esther resented Linnie, obviously. "I be trained to care for white child'en," she complained. But if Linnie was an offense to her pride then she would have to take her pride and protect it under a roof other than the one where Linnie's mother paid the bills.

"Why, oh no, Miss Geneva, I don't resent little darky boys, where you ever get such a idea ? Why, I worked here ten long years for good pay, and I wouldn't want to quit on account of your little adopted child."

So once Mildred Esther was brought under control, she was very solicitous of Linnie. She stood and handed him objects to throw until he tired of it. The hired help learned that the new little adopted boy was to have his way no matter what. Geneva never wanted him thwarted.

When he began to walk, he discovered the basement steps, where he liked to throw glass bottles from the top and listen to them crash against the stone floor at the bottom. This pleased the youngster so much that he used up all the bottles they could find in the house, and Geneva was seen out at the city dump collecting more bottle for him for his pleasure. Glass piled up in the basement at the foot of the steps and Andy had to sweep it up in the evenings and carry it back to the dump.

Two other blind children whose parents Geneva knew casually were invited in as companions for Linnie. Test cases. To see how Linnie interacted with others. But Linnie, large and strong for his age, threw the youngsters around as if to see what kind of noise they made when hitting the walls, or wrestled them in a blind, seeking, unheeding way, touching them like pieces of fruit and slinging them from his way as he went. He was terrible. No one would come near the house now.

He loved riding the city bus, but in time people knew what to expect, and as soon as they saw him getting on, they would get up, all would stand and get off as if escaping with their lives.

Yet not a word would Geneva hear against her son. She would not stand for jealousy and resentment and hatred of him. Naturally they must hate him. For wasn't he a beautiful, golden, dark-skinned thing? And didn't he have a wonderful singing voice? And how he played the piano! He was really superior the way her future husband had been superior, which was the only kind Geneva would fool with; didn't they know that by now? Didn't they know that nothing less would do for her?

Next to his music, Linnie loved to ride his little pony. He named it Winston. The pony was kept in the old stable and the garden was used as an exercise lot. Her Linnie rode in wild circles, hanging on to Winston's neck like a cat, his mouth thrown open in wild delight, screeching madly, as he drove the creature on and on in a cloud of flying dust.

"He don't know he can't see," Mildred Esther told people. "He think everybody like he is."

"Oh, how in hell can he not know something like that? Don't you people up there at the House talk about seeing with your eyes?"

"He don't listen to nobody no matter what they say. But Miss Geneva don't let you even mention colors nor nothing for fear he'll get mad or sum'um. And he never goes around, nobody that can stand him long enough to talk to him."

"Well, if that isn't the dumbest thing I ever heard tell of," people said.

"I sure thought Geneva had more sense than that."

"She do. It's just laying low. The minds of humans act like that sometimes. Disappear in the darkness and sleep like a polar bear."

"Wonder what kind of mind that little Linnie boy really has. What kind of pictures travel in his head if he don't know about color. His mind and hands and body are never still. I think of his thoughts as a whirlpool of great black and white ribbons swirling in the air like an ocean. But that can't be, because black and white are colors too. Maybe it's just words in his head, words and sounds like great flocks of birds darting and screaming all day."

"Close your eyes and try to imagine what it's like being blind."

"Close them for years like Geneva has and then you still won't know."

"What do you mean by that?"

"What do you think I mean?"

Although it was true the boy lived fairly isolated from others, he did not seem to care. In fact, this seemed his preference since he had many activities that claimed his time. Geneva he looked upon as a mere instrument of his will, someone to do as he instructed, and his only concession to her was from time to time allow her to hold him in her arms or smother his face with kisses when he did particularly well at a piano recital.

Otherwise he considered his life a very superior one and had no recognition or hint that others possessed a normal and wondrous sense that was absent in himself. Yet there were moments of unease. Times when Geneva had a scare, such as the morning when Linnie was practicing on the grand piano they had just moved to the east windows.

There the fierce sun rose in summer over the treetops and flooded straight into his face. Geneva heard him stop playing and saw him rise and advance slowly to the windows with his jaws falling lax in a kind of intense suspicion. There he stood a long time in this stunned, questing manner, as if almost in contact with the great secret she kept from him.

It seemed he stood this way for half the morning, swept by an acute state of suspense for something in the heat, a mystery pouring out of the fatal darkness through which he stumbled like a mad man under the moon. Geneva's heart pounded as she watched this. It was better to keep the windows covered from now on. About this time the Todds held their annual festival along their river park. Geneva had kept up connections with Leonard's family until she had Linnie, then she was too busy being a mother to involve herself. Now, this year she and Linnie, who was eleven, but overgrown to the point where he appeared more like fifteen, would attend, for there were horses to ride and a dance band in the evening. There was a wooden floor constructed especially for the dancers, with a bright canvas tent over it and a lot of festive streamers fluttering everywhere in the air.

It was here, in this bright and cheerful park that Linnie met Zootie Cat Bird Napier. Zootie was twenty years old and he cared for nothing in this world but a good time. And he got plenty of good times from what they said about him. Life to Zootie was a great joke, the joke of jokes he couldn't stop grinning about. He drank and played cards and ran where he wanted. He was one of the best dancers in any crowd, and he danced and jitterbugged in all the bad roadhouses with any kind of woman who came in the door and could keep up with him. Everyone knew him and adored him for his big blue eyes and curly hair, and handsome shape, no matter how badly he behaved.

Geneva had seen him around for years. She had negative feelings about him, a superstitious dread that he was lying in wait for her somehow, ready to pull her down into the uproar of his life. It was a foolish feeling, of course.

Once when he was working in a shoe store she had gone there. A young woman had come in with a little boy and Zootie, just for fun, brought him out a pair of men's shoes for him to try on. He put them on him. "There, God damn it, you're a man now!" Zootie declared. And when the child refused to take the shoes back off and cried, Zootie let him walk out the door in them, shuffling and stumbling. "Let him wear what he wants to, he's a man now. Nobody's business what a man like that wears!"

Another time he had a job driving a taxi cab for the city. Down the street in front of Welner House he sailed one morning in a taxi splashed over with mud and stuffed with fifteen country people he had collected from the back hollows, bringing them all to the eye clinic in one load.

His face had a reckless, confident look. He was always red from a few drinks and grinning. He frightened Geneva.

Later on, some of his buddies got him on at the fire department. Fighting fires. He had worked there two weeks when the mayor's house caught fire — not a real fire, actually — just a lot of smoke from where the housekeeper had left an iron on the ironing board and it was scorching and filled the house with smoke. But Zootie and his buddies, who were no better than he was when they were around him, rushed in with axes and fire hoses and wrecked the house from top to bottom. Flooded it. "Take your axes to those doors, boys, chop 'em down. Somebody might be trapped in the walls!" Zootie yelled.

Not only was he fired from this job, but he got himself thirty days' observation at the local asylum.

He had been out two months when he met Linnie at the riverbank festival. Soon as Linnie heard Zootie talking, he was drawn to him in fascination and wanted to hang around with him. "Why, hey, boy, you can't do that!" Zootie roared. "You're a nigger!" The crowd grew silent. But the remark went flying over Linnie's head. He had no idea of its meaning, and laughed in innocent delight and excitement, stumbling and groping to stay near Zootie's voice.

Geneva left the festival grounds early, half-dragging Linnie, who whined and resisted and wanted to know everything about Zootie Cat Bird.

For the next two weeks he kept it up, talking of nothing else. "Why can't I see him again? Why can't we go see him for a visit? I could have fun with him. He could teach me to dance like he does and go around where there are people, not like here, with your old victory waltzes from the First World War and crap! So why can't I?"

"Because you can't, that's why," Geneva said firmly. "Your Zootie is crazy!"

"You're the crazy one!" Linnie shot back, and struck out into the air as if to hurt her. Geneva was startled into a trance of disbelief. Had he actually meant to strike her? Hurt her?

"Oh, come on now, honey," she consoled him, "Let's go over to the Y and have a little swim. That will make you sleepy. Then we'll have a sandwich and you can take a good nap and then practice your piano."

"I want to see Zootie Cat Bird, that's all I want! I want to or I'll break my piano!" Geneva was frightened. She had seen his fits of rage before when he couldn't have his way, and she knew there was no sense in talking to him. He was down on his knees looking for something angrily. His hands fell on the hammer which he kept. He liked the hammer and the noise it made. He began to tap the piano keys with the hammer. Lightly at first, then harder. The piano was very expensive.

"Oh, don't! Don't do that!" Geneva screamed. Linnie threw the hammer against the wall and it smashed into the mirror and broke it. The mirror collapsed in tiny pieces. Geneva began to cry. "Oh, please, please, darling, no! No! Sit down, calm yourself. We will get Zootie on the phone. I promise. I'll have him come over here. He stays in some house over in Walkertown, I think. With relatives or something. Oh, God, I haven't kept up with the young people. They don't interest me, never did in fact." She felt herself half-writhing, on the edge on an explosion. "He imposes himself. Does things," she muttered.

"What kind of things? I bet he has fun! These people around here never laugh or dance. Go on, call someone and get his number. I want Zootie to take me dancing!"

And so that weekend Zootie came to pick up Linnie. Geneva was sure he would be hours late and prepared Linnie so he would not be anxious. But Zootie was early, in fact.

He was dressed in a negligent way with his face red as a fire plug and smelling of liquor. He was in a high, joking mood and it didn't bother him at all to ask Geneva for fifty dollars. "Just a loan," he said and fell into his wild laugh, showing his white, even teeth. Linnie was dressed and eager. He climbed into the seat next to Zootie and they drove off at high speed, nearly hitting a small dog crossing the street, leaving it yelping in terror.

By midnight they had not returned.

Geneva tried to lie down and rest but she could not. Her eyes opened wide for each car that came down the block. Then to her surprise she realized she was asleep and that the doorbell was sounding far down the stairs and hallways.

She jumped up and ran into the front lobby to see Caroline in her robe letting in two men, tall and thickly-set, whom she recognized as local policemen. Her heart began to pound wildly. They were looking around as if to take note of everything, for they had not had the privilege until now of seeing inside Geneva's home.

They kept on their hats.

"Ginny, I'll be fast with this news," the first one spoke in a low voice of confidence. "You should never, never have turned Linnie out with that Napier boy. He's done a terrible thing."

"What? What terrible thing!"

"Took him over to the next county and had him confess to the rape and murder of several white women, that's what."

"I don't believe Linnie would confess to something like that!" Geneva's eyes darting from face to face.

"Well, he has. 'I'll confess everything,' they said Linnie shouted, while this Zootie roared with laughter. They took over the jail, I hear. Now the sheriff over there across the line got his signature. And when I tried to talk to him, telling him what a bunch of foolishness this all was, he just put his feet up on the desk and shook his head, saying in that off-putting voice Deaton's got, 'You know I can't do nothing to help you now.' I know Sheriff Deaton. They've got a law down there that gives the death penalty for shooting cows. I'm not kidding you. They tried to hang a man for killing an old cow in a hunting accident once. He said to me in that dumb voice of his, shaking his head,'Now. He signed it. What's an officer of the law supposed to do when someone comes in here and wants to confess something like this?'"

The man looked as he talked from Geneva to Caroline, who stood with her hair flattened in a thick white net next to Geneva's shoulder.

"The...the Lord have mercy!" Caroline whispered in outrage.

"But I'll tell you," the officer went on, "our people here in the police station...we don't think it a bit funny. We arrested Zootie soon as he crossed back over the county line in his car. We got to talk to you some more, Ginny. This problem with Linnie. It's been swept under the rug just too long now. You've got to do something."

Do something! What more could she do! What on earth could she do now?

The officer held his hat, changed it from one hand to the other, then put his arm around Geneva. "They're bringing Linnie home. Miss Geneva, listen to me. He knows now." Geneva's quick eyes stared at him as if begging him to say no more. "He knows about his eyes and how it all happened. He's very quiet about it. Zootie's a blabbermouth; you knew that when you let Linnie run with him."

Geneva began to weep. "My heart is broken. Broken on his pain." She wept, collapsing into a chair where she remained the rest of the night.

So Linnie came home. He went out back and fed his pony. He played his piano and bathed. But he refused to speak to Geneva. His face frightened her. He seemed almost bloated with angry hatred; it pushed and pressed against his cheeks. She felt if she touched him or spoke he would go off like a can of gasoline.

In the middle of the third afternoon he went insane. He took his hammer to the furniture, to the piano. When Geneva arrived home, she was in fear. The house was dark as if everyone had fled it.

Only the small light above Dr. Todd's portrait still gave off its gleams, but now showing a large angry slash across the face. Geneva stood in the middle of the darkened parlor. After a while she imagined she could hear breathing — quick, angry breathing. Carefully she turned on a small hall light, and there sat Linnie, sprawled in exhaustion from the destruction, his face a rage of hatred. He could feel her in the room. He sprang towards her, towards her screaming throat.

"Lord, honey, he try his best to kill Miss Geneva." Mildred Esther told everyone. "He blaming her for his eyes being gone and all. And they took him away. Yes'um, but it took all of fifteen men to put him down and get him stropped. He fought 'em like a tiger, honey. They couldn't quiet him for nothing. He's been over there for days at that state hospital and still can't do a thing with 'im. Every time they mention Miss Geneva's name it start him up again."

Mildred Esther carried a nice lunch tray up to Geneva each day, knowing how Geneva was just coming out of the laying down sickness and had to be treated right. Petted. Yes, she needed to be petted. "So don't you take on about it so much, honey, " she soothed, "for I don't know what people expect out of a boy like that Zootie Napier, being who he is and all. With a mother like Gracie Washburn. What can a body expect?"

"What did you say?" Geneva stood straight up on the floor, spilling the tray with all her food, and stood with her mouth wide as if seeing her fatal destiny revealed and established before her eyes.

"Why, nothing. I don't know what I'm saying at times. I didn't say nothing." Mildred Esther replied so rapidly and honestly that Geneva seemed to believe her, and sat back down in her chair and began to weep again, as if that was all she must do now, for that was all she could do, that and nothing more, until the last tear was wrung from her eyes and she could start her life all over again.

Visions and Burdens

MAN IN BED 13A LAS VEGAS, NEVADA

I must have been looking down until the last second for what I remember is the feet of the people, all kinds of shoes. Then, just before we were hit, feeling how the air changed, a sudden gush of air lifted and swirled the fine blonde hairs on the girl's neck in front of me. Her wild sweeping arm gesture startled me as she arched her back, screaming, clawing at the sky. All those shoes flying off.

Hey, look, I know cars can't fly. I know they can't swim, either. But in my sullen dark sleep I seen this one off the ground. Sometimes she's driving it upside down, parting the foaming water just to get at me it seems, the car aimed at us like a rocket. And then she hits us, carrying me backwards, dropping me down like a mouthful of spit.

Somehow imagined I had yet to be picked up. They kept walking past me. Picking up the others.

Taking them away in the ambulances, but not me. Overlooking me on purpose. Why did they pretend I had been thrown so far from the others that I couldn't be located or calmed?

I belong to the others. I want to be included. In the hospital a cruel, dangerous yearning to meet these others took hold of me, so as soon as I could bear the pain I eased myself into a wheelchair and wheeled off down the hospital corridors, my hand firmly extended, introducing myself all around to patients as if we were now bonded forever by the event...like the Jews and their Holocaust.

I wanted to know their names, get their phone numbers. All about them, for we all stopped at the same instant.

We almost died together. We...

Even that young couple on their honeymoon — I did't leave them even for meals. If they had visitors in their room I remained present, assuming a place in their lives now. I will never let any of this be forgotten; "I nearly died in that accident," I told another man, who had mentioned my Blue Cross insurance, laughingly saying, "I sure hope you are paid up like I am." As if all the hardships of modern violence can be taken care of with an insurance card. A piece of plastic. "Look at my face," I told him, "at my jaw that hangs out like a broken drawer. My teeth smashed out. The blood I had to pull out of my throat in strings." I stared at him with the cold intention of letting him know we are all in this together, forever. He will never escape this, none of us will.

The nurse came and spoke to me. She stared down at me. "Mr. Lewis, I don't know how to say this, but...the other patients are complaining about you. Saying you're worrying them out in the halls. Soon as they see you, they hobble off in the other direction, or haven't you noticed?

"The doctors too are puzzled by your excesses, coming at them with all your showdown questions. You might get moved to another ward. For harassing everyone.

"What is it you want from them?"

I would like some soul like mine
carried on the wings of fate
his pain made golden with a song
that finds some meaning in this wrong.

"Nothing," I tell her. "I want nothing."

A woman from the apartment where I lived came to see me. "Why won't you see your girlfriend? She's crying all the time."

The woman had her daughter with her. Her daughter had her two friends. They turned pop cans up to their heads and drank, studied me with their big cow eyes slanting over the rims of their pop cans, looked at me sideways. One suddenly bent forward as if I were something at the far bottom of a well.

"I can't get over that accident," I told them. "I don't even know the people's names who died. I wanted to write down their names. No connection to me now — it's all dropped out of the news completely...except these dreams are with me yet. These dreams start out so smooth. Like the calm, neon-spangled town you see out our window here at dusk. You know when you walk up to the windows and see the city through the thick air-conditioned glass, so thick and chill you can't hear the city itself. Like a carnival seen from a distant hill, a view without music or sound of any kind. But I know something is going to happen.

"Something is coming. I feel the air moving, then the sound breaks in, jarring me like I'm hit by a train. I try to run but my legs turn to stone, then I'm smashed against the street. I wake up sick. My hands reach to see if blood is draining out of my mouth."

The women stared at me. "You never used to be such a gloomy bastard, Mr. Lewis," the woman said.

Then there came the day of the party. The little cross-eyed woman who changes the light bulbs emptied the waste, came shouting out about a party. "There's going to be a going-home party!"

She had a cartful of discarded light bulbs, hundreds of them. Like little fragile white skulls.

"Everyone who was going to die from the accident has died," she cried.

"So everyone else is now safe! Even you, Mr. Lewis, with your crushed forehead. Your skull had to be sawed all the way around, then lifted like a little beach house upon stilts. You kept crying out for me to come drive the flies off your brain. Remember that? And now you're well and there's going to be a party. And the news cameras! Come on, Mr. Lewis, everyone is going to sign each other's casts. You should not sit here brooding!"

PART II: WINGS BEAT AT THE GATES OF FATE

The Man in Bed 13B

Soon as I saw the new patient I wanted to wake him. Start slamming my mouth to him about the accident.

Some things you cannot control. They had brought him in about three in the morning. And he was still asleep. I kept walking over to him to look down at his face. A tall dark man, too tall for the bed, so his feet were sometimes propped up on the footboard, then they swung down off the side of the bed. Elbow bent across his face, breathing heavily through his lips. At last I bend and tug gently at his shoulder, lightly, until his eyes open, startled by a face bending so close to him in a strange place he doesn't recognize.

"What do you want?" he shouts. Then he jumps out of bed and looks around with wild, confused eyes. "What time is it? They took my watch. This here our sink?" He walks about, rubbing his stomach. "My stomach. Christ, I haven't eaten in days. They took my watch. I need a match. You got my ashtray? "

I look at him.

"No, I don't have your ashtray. You got my refrigerator?"

"All I want is a cigarette. You got a match? Bathroom down the hall? What the hell time is it? One-thirty? In the afternoon? You mean in the afternoon? Is it morning or what?"

Long bare feet on the floor, muscular legs exposed from his wrinkled hospital gown. He goes to the sink and begins splashing water over his face. His hands tremble as he dries his face and combs his hair, black as lacquer when wet.

"Look at this," he tells me, holding out his hand to show how it trembled with a thin, ungovernable, convulsive quiver.

I stare at him. "Were you in that same accident as the rest of us?"

"Accident!" he scoffs. "What accident? You call that an accident? Three days ago you know where I was? In a delirium!" He runs the comb through his hair. Several rapid strokes.

I see he is a talker. "In a delirium?"

"Yes. But in another part of the hospital, having a delirium! Yes, a delirium...but it was the medication they were giving me. I was under arrest, you see. My connection with the event got me in trouble. The medication went bad. Began to feel slow waves traveling up and over my body. Over and over, these waves... the doctors couldn't stop them. Had this cut place here on my leg, just below the knee.

"And each time a wave came to this cut place, guess what would happen? It would stop, hesitate, catch on fire.

"Glow icy-blue hot, like a thought you hate to have, like it was bursting into flame. I almost went out of my mind. I started to scream, 'I can't stand my leg! Can't stand my leg!'"

He lifts his gown and shows a jagged cut, a mass of black stitches splashed over with red disinfectant.

"That accident was bad on a lot of people," I tell him. "All those people like flies bouncing off a light bulb."

"Yes, that so-called accident was hard on a lot of people, that's for sure. But I just wasn't one of them.

"In fact," he says, his face in rapt gratitude, "I was saved by that incident. That event was my salvation!"

"I think you mean you survived it."

"No. I cannot claim that. Not yet. "

He continues after a moment. "My situation was different. Unbelievable different. I was involved in the event. Yes. But my involvement was private...because I wasn't exactly present at the scene."

"Where the hell were you then, eating fried chicken in Barcelona, Spain or something?"

"I was standing five floors up, facing my reflection in the hotel window overlooking the main drag of Vegas. I had been up there a long time. All night. Locked in alone. Something horrible had happened to me. I was ready to die."

"You were going to jump? Kill yourself?"

"Yes, jump. I was going to jump out the window. It was an awful feeling."

"I can imagine."

"It was my gambling."

"We all come here to gamble."

"Yes. I know that. But I had wasted my company's fortune. So I was going to jump. At ten o'clock A.M.

"Nothing was going to stop me! I had the alarm clock set. I had it set behind me on the table, for ten o'clock, a signal I would obey without hesitation when the time arrived. You see, fate has always served me from the sidelines, you might say.

"It is hard to explain." He sat down and combed his hair some more. He was silent for a long time, then he said, "But you see, I was a prodigy. You know what a prodigy is? I could do complicated math at two years old. Play Mozart at four. Something great was supposed to come to me. But nothing ever did. I was fourteen years old and burnt out. It is strange, but all these years something down in me has been waiting, clamoring, clamoring to be elevated, like a kid crying to be lifted up to a window to see. It's like an ache, pushing at me, my old self.

"Like something big is going to happen at last. Well, back in March, I came out here and the mania was on me again. Like something big was going to happen at last.

"Passing the casinos I felt something enormous was again within my reach.

"I looked good in my clothes that night.

"That's what started it off, a little thing like my straight black hair lying the way I like it. Had on a tux.

"Nails scrubbed, evenly clipped. I take pride in my looks, my physique, and this pride spread to others in the room that night. I could feel it. The way they looked at me, as if a switch had been thrown, starting up a low-chill current of excitement. A crowd came and stood by my elbow as I started to win.

"Then, for the next five hours I was taking this town. I could feel my brilliance stuck in me all these years beginning to fireball."

"What do you mean, 'stuck in you'?"

"Well, it's possible to have intelligence but not the capacity, biologically speaking, to use it. To have it stuck in you. Like with the dolphins, to use an extreme case. They have intelligence, but not the biological means with which to develop it."

"Yes, it looks that way. Like all they know is fun."

"Ha, yes. But for us we know...we know what fun costs. They were suddenly leading me somewhere...into the fresh air, across the back streets. I was like a fish hooked by the mouth.

"Remember just a vague picture...a pair of shiny sharkskin shoes walking around the room. A voice went with the shoes. Not my problem to tell the company. Let an undertaker tell them. I hate small talk myself.

"The owner of the shiny shoes sent me out of there in a taxi, back to my hotel.

"In the hotel room was a case of liquor. Ordered especially for the victory party. I had been that certain of victory!

"Now all was lost. Pension funds. Treasury bills. Bonds. Even the change in my pocket went to the taxi driver. Once inside my room I ripped open one of the cases and stood with the bottle tilted to my head. I had not had a drink in five years.

"The first long swallow ran everywhere in me, transforming me at once.

"I could feel it splash over my trembling lips and teeth. Into my throat, into the poised muscles of my back and calves, to the very roots of my hair. Spreading like a little fire in sweet blinding diminution, into the bottomless pit of my pensive life.

"The grief inside me was static now, bearable until the time came to jump. It was now eight-thirty in the morning.

"I checked the alarm clock. Death was fixed on its face. Death was time and time was the alteration of whiskey inside the bottle. I never looked at the clock again. I drank in quick, sharp sips, trying to reach a climax of intoxication before the alarm went off. But the climax would not come; only the heaviness eased me, and I stood like a horse gone to sleep in its harness. Weaving before the window in a daze.

"Beyond the city lay the great, toneless, spreading desert and blue rolling mountains bolting forever into the sky.

"For a long time I stood this way. Hardly realizing the sun was striking the roofs and that half-consciously my eyes were looking at something moving. My drunken eyes were following a car.

"An old battered-up job. Ascending into sight off the desert."

"Ha! I know who that was!" I cry.

"Yes, it tantalized me. The way it was going around and around the streets. Provoked pursuit. I had to follow it. When it went from view, I tore the drapes off the window to keep it in sight."

"Yes, I used to think about her when I was in intensive care," I tell him. "I had the nurses read the newspapers to me about her. And I could imagine her driving out of the city...Buffalo, New York, it was, heading for us across the looming thruways, the wind shaking the old car to pieces. Half asleep on some song she's listening to. I don't know why I have this picture of her. "

"Buffalo? I read she was from New Hampshire." the man says.

"She was. But her husband was from Buffalo. It's hard to keep it straight without writing it all down. Her husband was ill. He had been stuck on a kidney machine for years. And when he died she went there to Buffalo because she wanted to see where he had grown up. Walked around the snow-packed streets under the big elm trees there, secretly watching the boys playing hockey as her husband had done. Started showing people his pictures, a school photograph of a kid in a soccer uniform. Asking everyone if they knew him."

"I never think of Buffalo."

"It's an old canal town," I tell him. "One of those old salted-down outposts on the Great Lakes, crumbling to rust. The railroads cut through it ever which way. I was there once, laid over on my way to Canada."

"Well," the man continues. "I was up in the window, looking down. Watching this car. Driving in this erratic way. Then it happened. It rocketed...went into the open center lane of the main drag. It surged, almost alive. Heading straight towards those people on the crossing.

"*She's going to lay those people down*, I thought in that crazy lucidity drunk people can have.

"It knocked me completely awake.

"I forgot all about jumping out the window. But you know, the weirdest thing is this: just at that very instance the alarm clock went off on the table for me to die! The sound exploded like dynamite. I grabbed at the thing but fumbled. I must have looked like a starving man in the wilderness trying to catch a screaming chicken.

"Anyway, I dropped it and it rolled out of reach under the bed. You know how hotel beds are fastened to the floor and can't be budged. I swore at the clock and when I looked again I saw the car had cleared the street of people and was slinging them around like they were attached to a clothesline.

"I ran for the stairs, falling several times, nearly going over the railings. Behind me the clock was still ringing like it had yet to let anyone down. I had wound it that tight! It belonged to my family, an antique piece of junk.

"Into the street I went, breathless. I could see blood spreading everywhere.

"I stood there gasping, my back pressed to a wall. This could be me, splattered on the ground! My eyes filled with tears.

"The police were all around, traffic stopped. People screaming.

"They were pulling the woman out of her car. Throwing her back against the side of the car. Cursing her, jamming her back."

"You saw her?"

"Face to face. Yes. Fate rolls in the fog like a bell. You know from the papers she was from a wealthy family. And that she had broken down after her husband died. He had a horrible disease of some kind that kept him attached to tubes. And she had sat by his side for nine years.

"And she looked it.

"She had this queer, thin plainness certain rich women have. A queerness. A certain lame servant girl melancholy that fascinated me. A silent, unpeaceful female strength I have seen before in loners. So she was like that .Hidden away, taking care of her husband. Well she looked it to me, like I said. Like something that has lived out of the light, even her hair... her hair with this somber blondeness, like the light around... certain apples...you know, apples picked hard and green and forced to ripen in the dark, forgotten in drawers or cellars.

"The ghostly perfume of them.

"I looked at her pale face, but her eyes shot away from me, hard as two iron bolts. I ran on foot after the police car with her in the back seat. I knew I had to see her again, speak to her, touch her in some way.

"So the next day I went to the holding center and told them I wanted to see her.

"It was a dangerous thing to do.

"The officer in charge was a rough, sluggish sort. He looked at my messed-up tux.

"'You a lawyer?' he asked.

"I nodded. I was holding my breath, my heart was really up there.

"For he rose and took me back through a chasm of iron gates to a concrete room, a grim little holding place with two metal stools and a desk, dank and smelly as an old urine-soaked city park. I waited for what seemed hours.

"Then the gates whined and opened with a hideous, crashing jar.

"I looked and saw her coming in a narrow tunnel of a walkway, walking silently next to a blunt-faced female guard, the sun crossing and coursing on their faces as they passed the barred windows.

"I knew I had little time. The guard was already suspicious of my rumpled clothes.

"I put out my hand to the prisoner. I looked her straight in the face.

"I whispered her name: *Leanna. Leanna.*

" 'I needed to meet you. We had to meet. I had to see you...

" 'Had to tell you that your appearance here in this town —

"'That your appearance here in this town. It had an extraordinary effect on me.'

"The guard's face changed, like a shade going up on a window and she saw.

"She seemed to actually crouch down like a watch-dog that hears a key click.

"'Who? Who did you tell the people out front you were?' she asked. 'Did they make you sign anything?'"

"So that's how you got in here! The cops decked you! You've been in jail. For running after her, crying out your thanks to a mass murderer!"

"Well, it meant everything to me," he says.

"Just to meet her, to hold her gaze, to thank her for my life.

"I can't believe my luck!"

"No one ever believes his luck," I say, stretching and yawning. Soon I will be moved to another room. I sleep there in peace.

First Crime

I TRY TO LIVE ENTIRELY IN THE PRESENT AND ENJOY WHAT IS before my eyes. I am an ordinary woman who likes to clean floors and polish furniture. I can spend all day washing a refrigerator or an oven and never look up. Then once the job is finished I keep going back to it, opening the door and peeking in as if I want something inside when I only want to admire the clean shine I have put there. That's why I would be good for this job you have available. Cleaning your office after your clients have gone for the day. I like the look of an office with everyone out of it, everyone gone. Vacuous. All sound gone. Like now. Like a vacant stage... where performances have gone on during the working hours. All those problems people have dragged in though the door for you to mull over and ponder, little fates they want you to save them from.

Yes, I like to work. The only thing I don't like is ironing, although I used to love it. At one time I ironed everything: curtains, bed sheets, the Bible...although I am not religious in the least...I used to get up in the night and press the leaves of my Bible one by one...those delicate thin leaves...with a steam iron to make them smooth and perfect. Yes, back in the summer in all that heat, bent over an enormous round table, pushing that rabid steam iron back and forth, back and forth until I was hypnotized. That's why I stopped ironing...because it was leading my mind astray, making me ramble back and forth, back into the trembling past.

Counselor, I hate the past. The past is like looking down in your pants in public. Like stretching the waistband out from your waist and looking down there...very embarrassing and frightening because you never know where it will lead. The past can be a dangerous trail to step on. Yet everyone wants to go there, bring it up, and I guess I would too if I were in your position of hiring new help. Bringing a stranger onto my property from who knows where.

But you are accustomed to that, aren't you, being a district attorney. Questioning strangers. It is your job. You are one of these people who gets paid to find out all the evil in others and protect us from them. Some people are like that, born to know all there is in others...the diseases we've had, the shampoos we use, what makes us cough or cry out in our sleep. How many people we've killed. Excuse me for laughing; it's a little funny...all this just to sweep someone 's floor.

For what does it matter really? I'm just an ordinary woman despite my past, despite the rugged hard little hills I have had to climb just to live. Nothing fancy in my demands, which is why I'd want a job like this that pays almost nothing while demanding certain intimate requirements such as "*the applicant should be of a presentable appearance.*" I suppose you mean should be pretty, good-looking, huh? Hey, look, that's O.K. I've always said this old world has too much ugliness in it and ugliness is just one more factor we can add to the crime waves in America. Everyone so fat and pierced. Dirty. Strung-out on drugs. I see your point completely in wanting to look at something pretty cleaning up the place. But the money now...

A few things about people with money I can't understand. Some wealthy people can be extraordinary, giving to this and that cause, but when it comes to us little people, the first instinct to kick in is our slaveowner's mentality. We are alive only to be small, so they can feel their bigness. Nothingness and Being. Ha ha.

Well, I worked for wealthy people, so I know. I thought rich people would be interested in things, you know, ideas. The big problems of this world. Improving the lot of the poor, stopping war and that sort of thing. But their interests were always the same. Each other. Always each other.

Never, never about me. I wasn't allowed to stick my head up in the way. Don't let their personalities rise. That's first rule. I heard this said about servants once. Always their concentration was on each other. You see, I worked for several families at the same time. Ironing their best linens and polishing antiques. But my real specialty was carrying tales. Oh, I had to be discrete, let me tell you. Very careful. Jealousy over who hears what first was fierce. I knew it all, all the abortions. All the priests who stayed too long hearing confessions. Affairs. What the daughters-in-law said. That sort of thing. Shoplifting. Alcoholic breakdowns. Talk precious to their ears.

But once they heard about — me — I was no more to them than a little mouse who had walked into the middle of a glue trap. I must be flushed down into the sewer from where I had crawled. No one said "What's this story I hear about your stays in the women's reformatory? A year here and a year there?" No. I was just flushed.

Lucky for me, I had my own car. A little red sportscar that would do a hundred easy. I drove it like that, a hundred, sometimes a hundred and ten, just to see how high it could climb without rattling. I drove away then, all the way out to California. Knowing they were looking for me, wanting to get even for keeping secrets.

One day a letter came for me. I was shocked that they had found my address, but you can't get away from them, I guess. They have you charted like the paths of stars. However, it was a nice letter, telling me that so-and-so had a brother who was the new D.A. now and no doubt had a judgeship waiting for him. That's you the letter was talking about. They said you would give me a job if I came back. I said, "Sure he will, after they put me away for ten more years." Ha ha. I kept the letter and my mind kept coming back to it. I would get it out and read it over from time to time. That was five years ago.

So I began to work for myself then. Out in L.A. Taking care of crack babies, both black and white, that the state government took away from people and gave to me to watch and feed. I liked that, liked the money and the importance it gave me. I could go into places and buy a pizza or a pack of cigarettes and not have to worry about the check bouncing in my face the next day. Not that I smoke. You don't have to worry about that. I don't. Never did. But I buy cigarettes all the same. For their packages. The feel of the shiny cellophane around them. Just the looks of them. The cheerful way they are designed as if some big thrill is waiting.

I keep these cigarette packs all around my apartment. I like to just pick them up and look at them the way I do one of my knives. Or my guns. This one, this small one here...you don't have to look frightened. It's cock-locked... ha, what a name, huh? Cock-locked! I can spend all day cleaning and shining my guns. I know it's strange seeing a woman with a bag of guns, toting them around. But it makes me feel important just touching them, the way money makes a rich woman feel — like nobody else matters and nobody better mess with her. I don't like being looked down on. Laughed at. I remember the first time somebody laughed at me.

It was a long time ago. Back when I was a kid. Young kid. Very young. Not even four years old yet. You will think I am lying when I say that I was only three years old at the time. But it's the truth. However, I was tall. Always a tall kid. I think I must have been three, four feet tall and only three years old. Or so it seems to me when I look back.

We lived in one of those old, dead little villages in rural Nebraska, a tiny town with a railroad cutting through the middle of it, on the edge of a great, empty, wind-scrubbed prairie, a landscape so flat you could drive all day and not be any nearer your destination than to the nearest star in the heaven. Crushes the mind to even think about it, like a tiny bug crawling 'round and 'round the bottom of a bottle. Yet we had a post office. Couple of feed stores. A dingy old pharmacy with a video machine in the back.

Although there was a paved road, people still walked the tracks to meet the morning and evening train. I see it all again in a kind of blue streaking smear, like a view from inside a speeding vehicle.

There was the small house — where the old couple lived. Two tiny people, all dried-up like a couple of corn shuck dolls. Neighborhood pets, really. Pets of the entire village, which looked after them with the pride people take in such things. The women spoke of them in a tender, rendering way, asking each other if they had stopped to see Aunt Sylvia and Uncle Levi today. Everyone wanted in on it, to pay their respects, climbing the rickety, unpainted steps and sitting on their hard chairs. It made the time pass faster for the two old people, they said.

The house was built up on stilts so the porch was almost level with the train windows when the train went by with strangers in them, waving. Of course they were related to everyone, it seems. Even to me. My mother was one of the women who went often to visit. It was a social thing; only the best women visited, taking food, bread they baked. Tomatoes and beans from the garden. Life crept along.

Well, like I say, I was very young. And I am sure you are aware how the minds of children are often like the minds of insane people. People try to tell them things and they don't understand. Then they do. So the growing up process is just a process of becoming sane. Of getting well, in a way of speaking. The insane, please notice, often have minds like children, minds that have not grown, childish minds, stunted. I'm sure you will agree. As if life is yet to be experienced, still to be explained, but remains forever absent in them no matter how long they live or what-all they do. I was one of those kids whose mind was like a mad person's and needed to grow.

Unusual ideas came to me. I believed, for example, that to kill was something only adults were allowed to do. Just because they were adults. Like on television. You never saw a kid killing people. So it would be wonderful to be an adult and kill people who offended you.

One day this mind decided on its very own to go see the two old people and pay them a visit as an adult. I dressed in my mother's high heels, purse and apron, for I wanted to feel the full dignity and importance of such a visit. I wanted to carry them something nice like I had seen the grown women do, and see the look of gratitude pour out of the old faces when I placed this before their eyes. I decided on a jar of pickled herring my mother was keeping for the holidays. And perhaps a pumpkin as well. It was autumn, and pumpkins were all over the place.

I picked a rather large one. Too heavy it turned out, a terrible burden to lug half a mile dressed as I was. Can still see it. Sweat pouring off my face by the time I reached their yard. Passed the old wind-warped picket fence with its mat of creeping morning glories. Climbing the steps, panting with these offerings.

I waited for the old smiling faces to appear, but, lifting my eyes, saw instead Sylvia gleaming from the top steps with sarcastic delight at my visit, and yelling for Levi to come see what had come up the road. They both stood looking down at me, laughing, blown over by such a comic sight, their old toothless jaws going like two horses biting at the bits.

I came confidently on up the steps and inside, placed the pumpkin on the table and took the jar of herring out of the large purse. The herring would please them. "Here, Aunt Sylvia, my mother sent you a very expensive present," I said in a loud voice. "I bet you never had herring before, did you?"

"What's this?" Sylvia asked sneeringly, studying the label. "More garbage to throw out. Why can't you people stop bringing in crap for us to eat?"

I looked around for a dish and fork so I could give them a taste. The place struck me now as very different from when I came with my mother. The atmosphere seemed unfriendly. Dingy and gloomy. The old woman swept over to the window where she could read the label on the jar better. As she moved she filled the place with a cloud of sour odors fanning out about her dresses, for she wore twenty or more of these garments and kept them on for years.

The two watched me fork out the neat hunks of fish into the saucer. They waited some time, standing in the doorway framed by the light. The old man had taken off his hat, and for the first time, I saw why he was never without it...he had a large sore on his forehead; inside the scab was a kind of dark hole like the path bored in by some filthy insect that slept there now in his skull cavity.

The old woman cautiously and suspiciously took the saucer I held out, forked a small piece into her mouth and chewed with a pensive look in her eyes. I stared at her, waiting for a great, pleasant reaction. Suddenly the strange scoffing look that had been playing around her mouth vanished, and she grabbed the jar to read again the label while spitting a mouthful back into her hand.

"You! You little..." she said, poking her face right into mine. "You're trying to feed me rattlesnake!"

"Rattlesnake!" the old man screamed. "Spit it here, Sylvie! In the stove!" He had lifted a stove cap on the cooker where he had a fire roaring. It flamed brightly crimson on the old woman's face as she gagged and spit with horror.

I don't know what made me want to attack them the way I did. I only know it became clear that a three-year-old out of pure revulsion can do a lot of damage. I vividly remember my flying feet coming at them then. My fists...feet...my fist...my feet! The old woman drew back in wide-eyed alarm, fanning her dresses about, wiping her mouth and saying something about being poisoned, and making wild, yelping sounds each time she was kicked, like an old turkey or rooster that knows it is going to die. I was not yet four, like I say, but very strong, and this strength was a great excitement to me.

I could run and leap and kick off the walls and run back at them, unfolding like a spring at every instant, punching and slapping at them as they made their raucous yelps.

The old man slung a chair cushion at my head then hurried, ran as if his only chance against death was to get up on the bed and kick at me by holding on to the headboard. The old woman had by this time thrown herself flat against the floor and spread her arms and legs like Christ on the cross, as if it were all over for her. Which of course, it was. But not yet. I saw her the next day, lifting her skirt before a crowd of women, showing off the blue places under her rags, then jerking the skirt back down as if something this terrible could be exposed only seconds at a time. "We didn't do anything to her. Nothing. It's just meanness. The meanness right in some kids."

I went back to their place a few days later, crept inside when they were napping and sat in the kitchen. Eventually the old woman came with a lamp whose light cast great shadows over the room and fell quietly on my face, waiting at the table. But what good were her screams now? They both died within hours of this second assault, and when everyone began asking questions, my mother took me away for a while. "You don't have to tell anyone," she said. "Not what they were trying to do to you. Old people are like that. Young children don't know. You are innocent. Innocent. You don't have to be upset."

I wasn't upset. Why should I be? I remember leaving their place afterwards in perfect serenity, even turning back and retrieving the pumpkin, lifting it, leaving the place filled with their gasping breaths, the old man sitting on the bed, pointing and shaking his finger at me.

Back out I went along the tracks. I heard the train coming and placed the pumpkin on the rails and waited, knowing that soon the great slashing wheels would send it flying against the sky in a hundred pieces. Like all things must. Like all things will. Wouldn't you say? The great squirming cosmos itself flying apart, exploding in bloody pieces one day. Maybe right before our eyes, before our waiting faces, as if on a quiet and empty stage with two actors prepared for anything...or isn't that the way you see it? What do you say?

The Good in Men

OUR TOWN LIES 120 KILOMETERS BEYOND SARAJEVO, IN AN OLD railroad valley that opens up to the wide heavens above the jagged tops of a dense range of mountains. We are Serbs here — Slavs. A Slavic people. The town has always been Serbian, but during the last war, the last big one, World War II, the Germans occupied it with the collaboration of hostile minorities such as the Croats and Bosnians and the like, who surrounded it in the outlying regions, just as they do now.

You know what followed this occupation if you read a little. These neighbors astounded even the Nazis with their unhampered brutality towards the Serbs — who, so these neighbors claimed, had done a lot of meanness to them in 800 A.D. and had suppressed them and held them back from progress ever since. Only 1200 years ago! How can we forget in such a short time? People actually think like this!

They actually get guns and shoot each other over these vague mythical records of wrongs that happened hundreds of foggy years ago. So what is one to do? Sit with a finger down your throat to show the world how bad you feel about all this history that has landed at our feet like an avalanche of skulls and axes? I am sorry, but I don't have that kind of finger. And besides, I don't want to be bothered, I can't be bothered; it is too much.

Even dwelling on what the lunatics did in 1941 is enough for me, and that was only sixty years ago, mind you. Sixty years! I am but twenty-three years old and for me to imagine even half of what has gone on in my own little lifetime — is like trying to push the wet belly of some monster off my face in a dream.

So how can I begin to take in centuries...when before me is the present, the great rise and fall of the Soviet Union, the most powerful and extensive empire since the Romans. You already know that, of course, like you know they were on our side, the side of the Serbs. They protected the Serbs. We were their little brothers, so to speak, and their influence covered this quarreling region like a great white paw, keeping everything cool and quiet as a snowfall. The lid was on, so to speak. We could feel it all the time, this great paw ready to move and pounce on any hateful little minority that might want to start ganging up again on us.

But even before I was born this empire began to crack apart. People knew the big paw was wincing and drawing back under the relentless blows of the capitalist west. Naturally the Serbs grew nervous and started looking around for some way to protect themselves. They began arming themselves, hoarding guns and drawing up plans in order to "take precautions" against what had happened to them under the old Ustashi.

For myself, I couldn't bear hearing about it all the time. I was nineteen then, and wanted nothing but to study the stars. I wanted to be an astronomer. That was all I wanted. But everyone was eaten up alive with the past, insane with the long record of hate they carried around inside themselves. Learning something new was not a big fad.

Now you take men like Maladic Stonovitch. He was ten years old when the Germans came, rolled into town and started rounding up Serbs for their labor camps. The public square I cross each morning is where they held the hangings and the beatings, and of course there were always the gleeful little onlookers, those neighbors who had turned the Serbs in and stood around waiting to watch it all. It is the onlookers the victims remembered the most, not so much the Germans as these onlookers. These neighbors that the Bible tells you to love. It was all repulsive, but you should have heard Maladic tell it.

It was all like a great movie to him, a big classic that never dies. And the way he walked about in his thick boots with his red-hot jaws working as if fairly exalting in the foul cruelty done to him. He thought himself the thing, you could see that. Always inviting strange groups into this home in the dead of night to watch old war footage, films he has managed to collect; those ghostly, dismal black and white news reels of the occupation. The dark churning transport trains stuffed with their terrified human cargo. "*There go your own people! Your own blood and bone!*" Maladic would shout with the projector squeaking 'round and 'round. "And there, that's me. That's actually me, Maladic! I'm only twelve years old there, but see how the bastards are afraid of my looks. Even with my hands tied behind my back they are still worried about me! Look how they strike me, now! Now! See how I refuse to fall. Look how strong I am! How tall! They know my strength is needed, but they know I am dangerous, too. There I am again. What luck to have got hold of these films. The Germans filmed everything, like they believed everyone would cheer them someday."

And for this everyone naturally looked up to Maladic in awe. "Oh, Maladic has been through it, and he knows about them. Maladic knows what's what, I'll tell you."

That he knew what's what, I'll have to agree, for if you wondered what some Croat was doing in 1941, or some Albanian in 1903, you only had to go to Maladic there at the railroad station, where he was stationmaster, by the way, and put in your request. For there he would be in his little smelly office with its grim yellow light, pouring over old war records and archives like a divinity student over the plagues and lamentations in the scriptures, hoarsely explaining it all with his big body making wild jerks and jabs of disgust.

"Oh, Maladic is smart. A brainy type," they would say. "And the best kind of Serbian father. I admire a man who knows family is everything in this world. There is something grand about him, big bear such as he is. And with those delicate gold-rimmed glasses on, like the ones Trotsky wore, I trust him to see everything. Even microscopic things that the average person doesn't even suspect of being alive and squiggling in the human mind, if you understand what I am getting at."

"Yes, Maladic knows his history. He knows it like he knows the trains. I have seen him take his watch out of his pocket and, just by staring at it, cause the train to blow its whistle five miles away in the hills. Every day he does this. I've seen it, but never said anything. I admire Maladic."

It pleased the people to know their hero was fixed for life in this job that was at the center of all the new excitement. Here everything started, stopped, and started all over again. There was no way Maladic could lose his fine importance in this town, and he knew it.

For myself, I kept to myself, to my job at the bicycle shop. I was busy from morning to night, but snatched a few minutes when I could to put together my own motorbike, something I had been working on for months. Months just to get the parts. And finally, on the same day the shooting started in Kosovo, I had it out on the road and flying in a ball of dust. That's all I wanted in this world then. I wanted to ride in the night and look at the stars.

But the men in the town suddenly drew together in a dark plotting way and went off into the woods with guns. I knew without a word from anyone that I must join them. If I did not, the tormentors would have singled me out in a day or two — that's as long as it would take, and then you would see my Honda around, but not its joy rider, who would be in a muddy ditch somewhere with a hole in his head. Snatched off the seat like a robin by a pair of hungry claws.

I didn't have to guess who the district militia leader was. There Maladic stood in style, his big boots and shiny AK-47 on his shoulder, his large eyes dark and burning. He designated the cemetery as the spot for our first meeting. This cemetery is nothing. A small plot by the roadside, very old and unkempt, with no more than a dozen gravestones, all with the names of Stonovitch carved on them, lifting like serene hands out of a weedy morass of some ancient rose bushes and vines.

Maladic chose this spot, he said, because it contained the bones of Serbs who had outfaced the devils and sons-of-bitches in 1941. He bade us all kneel and pray and make promises to defend Serbian soil. "Here lie the bones of the brave," Maladic shouted in the black, moonless dark. "Here is my family. Family is everything to me. You who are young now will understand that fully before you die. Or you will understand nothing."

We said our prayers aloud and loaded the guns and ammunition into trucks and went down the road towards the mountain pass.

Four of Maladic's sons, all of them tall, silent youths of whom he boasted constantly and wanted to keep within his sight, were among the night fighters. Only his younger son, Troyan, a good-looking kid of seventeen, and by far his father's pick of his eleven children, was shunted off into another safer activity. This Troyan was allowed to plan a project almost right in his home. He was to destroy the big railroad culvert which the communists had built years ago when they laid a new railroad into the region. Nowhere around could you find a public building half as impressive as this culvert. It was over forty feet high, and full of sandy mounds washed in on the backwater floods from the river. Where the evening sun came in at its wide mouth it threw tall hawk-like shadows on the curved walls, and if you stood a certain way your voice bounced off the smooth, cold softness in eerie echoes that no one really wanted to listen to. It was powerfully and beautifully constructed, and Troyan and his group drilled it full of holes where explosives would go in case the men decided to blow it to hell and back.

From time to time the young people of the town had hung around this culvert. Then something bad would happen and everyone would avoid it for months, but now, to Troyan and his friends, it was like a brand-new discovery. They began to go every evening, burning a few tires and smoking, listening to their music tapes and radios. The girls came down, too — off the riverbank in a close, hesitant little flock, in their American blue jeans and sneakers, just to see the young men and watch them burn the tires. I knew Troyan pretty well. He liked to help me work on my bike and I taught him a few things and let him ride it as often as he wished. But he was not the natural loner I am, and tended to grow moody and brood like something lost if he did not have his friends around him.

Yet the moment he was surrounded by his gang, all his gloomy energy turned into a wild good time and no one could stop him then from being happy. He was crazy as they get about music, American rock groups, and especially Elvis who represented nothing less to him than the twentieth century with its wings spread, flying away in glory.

He was never allowed to play this music at home. Maladic considered the stuff full of vile corruption and the cause of all modern diseases. But down in the culvert where Troyan carried his tapes in a black suitcase with straps and brass buckles holding it fast like a case of explosives, the youths yelled and danced all they pleased, and called the girls, who drew back a little in doubt of the assertive blasting downbeat, and were content to just stand back and let the boys have at it.

"Go see how Troyan is getting on!" Maladic ordered me one evening, and off I went in angelic obedience to see what hell was being raised. There, as I came down the footpath through the willows, I could see the young men had formed a circle, clapping and tossing their hair and letting their cigarettes dangle on their lips as their hands lifted above their heads, while Troyan stood in the center in open shirt and loose trousers like a gypsy, his brown hair and lean torso swinging and lifting in the blaze of the burning tire. Oh, he was showing them all right, showing them how it was done. As I was watching him, as I came closer, I glanced around and saw this one girl looking at him as well. She had tears in her eyes, something that gave me quite a shock. The tears came out of her wide eyes and over her cheeks and across her mouth that was held tight and distorted with feeling. She looked very beautiful to me, and afterwards I kept thinking about her. The look on her face as she watched him kept coming back to me, like any secret disturbance will, and I knew then that if ever I had a love it would have to be a love born of sorrow and show in such eyes like this girl had. It made my head ache to go on thinking about her, all this on and on thinking was not good for me.

Her name was Merna. Merna Voyic. And she lived up at the state orphanage — a rambling old place just within walking distance of the town, up a long, rough road full of mud holes with trees hanging over it, dark as a tunnel. The communists had taken it away from a big landowner whom they executed, although he was supposedly connected to the family of Prince Philip of Greece, the one who is so good-looking and married to the Queen of England. Anyway, it was converted into a school and home for war orphans.

Merna was about seventeen. Somewhat odd looking. With fuzzy yellow hair that stayed short over her head and very soft-looking, just like a little chicken's. She was one of those cut-up types who might have passed for a happy creature, except there was no real glow in her large intelligent eyes, only a certain impatience and fear of something, as if she imagined life was going to get away from her, pass her by in a wink, and she would never know the feeling of having lived. She was always up to some funny business, some trouble to fill up the space where real life should be, so she was a problem for her teachers who loved her and even spoiled her, or so the story went.

None of them knew what ideas she might get into her mind next. Even when she was eight years old, for example, she and a couple of her friends got a hold of a Parisian magazine and began to study its slick pages when no one was around. They sent off an order to some of the shops who ran advertisements in the pages. They ordered coffee, lipstick, several cases of brandy and some books on the workings of the female body, which they told the shops to charge to Prince Philip's account.

The shipment actually arrived and had to be sent back, of course, but for months later talk went around about how the orphanage was looking for thrills on the state's money and those girls "up at the home" were allowed to play-act with lipstick all over their faces. Even now Merna wore a lot of lipstick. She wore it down to the culvert because she knew Tryon loved the sight of a painted mouth. Their friendship was not well-known; only a few people mentioned it, for they were not allowed to go walking about together. Then Troyan went off with the other soldiers and Merna Voyic stayed away from the town. People forgot about her.

Some months passed. Then a full year. Everyone was miserable. What happened then was later related to me by others, and later by Merna herself, in such minute detail that even a blind man might think he had actually seen it.

It was a cool spring day in March. Sarajevo was no longer pinned down under sniper fire, but still there was no peace to be had in the region. On the streets no one was speaking a word to anyone, yet behind the silence you knew there existed a shadow government and a Crisis Staff that would do as it pleased with the country. The trains were full of soldiers carrying guns, men from all the villages swelling the ranks of the new breakaway Serb Republic. There was talk that the Albanians were about to start a civil war with the central government and that if they did, they were going to be creamed.

On such a spring day, Merna Voyic went to the train station with a pink scarf fluttering on her head looking for a letter from Troyan Stonovitch. No one paid her any notice, except Maladic, who was heaving the stuffed mail sacks down to the platform to put on the arriving express. He stared directly at the girl with offended eyes. He knew why she had come and he wanted to insult her and send her back up the road in distress. "There she is," he muttered to a man nearby, "that worthless little fuzzy-headed thing from up there at the orphanage with her mouth painted red as a cat's ass." He watched her as she came and stood among the other girls who wrote to soldiers. They stood with that curious pose that had evolved among them during these months of serious fighting.

The pose consisted, first of all, of having on the best clothes they owned, washed and ironed without a wrinkle anywhere, and shoes polished like little mirrors, with arms folded and perhaps with one foot turned quietly out, the knee at an angle, as if they were about to start a dance. A few of the girls were really befuddled, ridiculous; you could catch them standing there as if fantasizing themselves into Idiotland, their chins elevated so their hair flowed back as the train came throwing the wind, and the whistle fell into the valley like the cry of some animal that wants to get you down and wallow you around.

Maladic continued to glance at the girl. He disliked her so much because he knew she must be ignorant of the powerful importance of family, not having one herself. It was impossible, he believed, for such a woman to therefore show the near reverence or awkwardness the other girls had for him as the father of so many good, strong sons. No doubt, she wanted Troyan to give her all his attention, send her presents and keepsakes and who knew what-all. Who knew what someone raised without a family might expect from this world.

Maladic was a long time bringing up the mail sacks. He had first to confer with some armed soldiers riding the train and give them the needed information he was holding. The crowd understood his importance and waited in a hush until finally he brought the sack, sorted the mail into little piles and began passing down the letters.

Sure enough, there was an envelope for Merna Voyic with Troyan's handwriting on it, just as he suspected, but he did not speak or lift his eyes to the girl as he reached it down to her. Maladic's color had risen around his neck and the girl was aware of it. She went straight to the window and tore open his son's letter with brazen impatience, reading it again and again in the yellowish sunlight dropping through the little dirty squares of glass. She had a smile on her lips as if to provoke his nerves just because he would not allow Tryon to wipe his feet on a thing like her.

At last she spoke and Maladic looked up to see what he believed to be a smart flicker of derision in her eyes. "I have a letter here from Troyan," she said, "and here is a part for your ears alone, Pappa."

"For me!" Maladic reddened with blind hostility. It was highly offensive to him to be spoken to like this, yelled at across a room.

"My dear Merna," the girl read, lifting her voice to stop Maladic from saying anything more, "This is the last letter you shall receive from me."

"That's wonderful!" Maladic scoffed with a large laugh.

"I cannot tell you too much as to why," she went on, holding up her hand to silence Maladic, which infuriated him, "except to say the bright sweetness I once felt for you, or for any woman, has been ruined forever by what I have had to witness these past weeks. This world, and the dogs walking around in it calling themselves men, makes me want to never touch another woman, I swear it! And Merna, I am afraid for you. I have told you before that you must not challenge men like my father. I have told you and warned you to keep away from him. Take my letters and say nothing. For, Merna, my own father is such a dog, as I have just mentioned. And if there is any good left in men you will be kept from him somehow. What do you think a man like my father cares for a woman? He would take a woman and tie her to a plow and think nothing about it, just like he did my mother."

Maladic had tightened to madness. The words hit his face like a blow from a fist. His eyes were staring directly at the girl's throat where the scarf was tied in a knot. Her skin was irritated and red from her reading, and her hair stuck out near her face like small oily curls of brass. He came towards her then, slinging the counter door up and seizing her head, scarf, hair, all in one enormous muscular grasp, and with the other hand, he snatched the pages of the letter, and began running her towards the stove in the center of the room with her screaming and fighting the best she knew how. "This! This is no letter from Tryon! Tryon would never send such trash in the mail, you red-ass bitch, you!" he yelled, kicking open the stove hatch and throwing the pages onto the coals that broke into an aroused flame and devoured the paper as if on command.

Without hesitating, his hand sprang a blow to her face, then another, with such solid force that blood broke from her nose. He continued to strike her, not caring how she screamed and fought until she fell and crouched on a bench against the wall, gasping for breath. Blood ran down and covered the front of her dress and a glistening red drop hung very still under one nostril like a raw strawberry.

So great was her terror now of Maladic that she did not even hear the noisy feet of the men walking across the floor. There were six or more of them and they stared without speaking at the sight of the half-addled-looking girl, wild with fear, choking and bleeding in the corner of the room. Maladic spoke out in his energetic voice. "Ha! Would you look at this girl! She came in here sniveling and trying to start something with me. Trying to start a big fight because she didn't get a letter from that Jorge Voinovitch character she has been writing to. Can you imagine anyone weeping over a jerk like Jorge Voinovitch? You know the guy I mean. You've seen him around with his leather jacket. Pushing that old Honda that's always broken down on the roads somewhere. Sometimes I think he rides it upside down just to look at the stars! I almost shot him myself once for getting under my feet. And now this!" he pointed to the girl who was trying to wipe her nose on the end of her head scarf.

"Leave her alone, Maladic!" Another scolding voice sprang out in the room. It was that of Myra Bockman, an elderly woman who used to go up to the orphanage and help out with the laundry and set mole traps in the grass and such like. "So what if she writes to Jorge! Isn't he a soldier, same as the others? And doesn't he deserve comfort from the girls back home same as any other fighting boy? I hear he's doing quite well for himself despite of how you poke your ugly fun."

She went up to Merna and helped the distraught girl to her feet and out into the cold air. Here Merna began to shake and sob in a kind of fit. Her dress was covered in blood and everyone hurried to get past her, to not notice, nevertheless she would not go home on the road, but insisted on taking the path through the woods. "Let me alone, let me cry," she said in horrible broken voice, and wandered about on the path, stooping to wash her face in the cold water of a stream and wring out her head scarf. Old Myra tried to comfort her, to at least get her to hush that shuddering moaning sound which reminded the old woman of days she had best not dwell on.

Once they reached the orphanage, Merna broke away and climbed the old back stairs of the servants' quarters and found her room and refused to leave it. When the women learned from Myra Bockman what had happened, they were terrified and kept the poor woman up all night discussing the catastrophe and swearing her to secrecy over and over as if it were impossible to put faith in anyone anymore.

In time Merna explained to them all how Maladic had coined the story out of the air about her writing to Jorge Voinovitch, rather than Troyan. She wept and wept as she talked, refusing to take even a sip of tea the woman brought her, or to let them touch her swollen face. From down below in their classrooms, when they were certain she couldn't possibly produce another tear from those poor black eyes, they would hear her break out again in fresh sobbing.

It was nearly a week later, one chill morning before daylight when a round moon shone a flood of light across the fields, that a man traveled out of the village towards the orphanage. He was riding a bicycle, one of those old-fashioned ones, the kind with thick tires that went lumbering and swerving around the holes in the road. He pretended to be delivering some medicine and to be taking his time until he was out of sight of the houses, then he went in a hurry, panting through his lips as he pedaled up along the stone wall in the moonlight. He could hear his own breath and his chest hurt him as it had done the past twelve years. He pedaled around to the back entrance where he alighted in a great nervous rush and went straight into the matron's room without knocking and began to shake her shoulder. "Monica?" he whispered. "It's me, Chester. Something has happened. Get up. Go wake Margaret and the others. You've got to be quick with this," he said. His clothes and hair gave off a heated dampness from his night ride. Monica had sat up and was looking at him. She could see he was shaking to pieces and after slipping on a robe and hearing what he had to say, she pulled a bottle of brandy from the wall somehow and made him take a drink. They were both pale as they went to get the others.

A few hours later they took the news up to Merna Voyic. The headmistress led the way with the other teachers following. Their faces were white, almost bluish with distress. One carried a tray with some water and glasses on it. They went into Merna's room, shut the door and locked it. "Get up, girl. Something dreadful has happened. You better get ready for some bad news."

Merna was already awake and sitting on the bed with her hands folded in the dark. Her eyes looked strange and beseeching. She stared at the women. The mistress went straight into the story.

"Day before yesterday Troyan Stonovitch shot his commander in the face and then turned his gun on his entire outfit when they tried to stop him from running."

Merna put her hands to her face.

"It's worse than you can imagine, my girl. For you know what a good army does when one of its own members betrays his comrades like this? The men were swift to take justice against the traitor's family. Yes, I am afraid so. They came into the village last night and killed the entire Stonovitch family."

"It can't be so!"

"It can be so and is. Every one of them. I thought old Maladic would have been spared, being who he is, but no. They said he had all kinds of excuses why he should be turned free but he got his throat slit just the same and his body thrown on the midnight freight train with the others."

Merna Voyic began to tremble and lie rigid under the covers now. The women brought her some hot tea and put even more blankets on her. "Please try to stop this awful shaking now! Stop it! Here, here! Nothing is going to hurt you if you keep your senses. Maybe a little whiskey, Louise, what do you think? Yes, go get the brandy. And, oh, Merna, thank God you were not writing to Troyan, but to Jorge Voinovitch, like Myra tells. Or you might be lying on top of that Stonovitch pile yourself and maybe all of us here with you as well. You understand. You must understand." The entire room was half frantic for a minute.

"And Troyan?" the girl screamed, pushing away the glass they held to her lips. "Troyan! Did Troyan escape? Did Troyan get away?"

"He did."

"But Merna," the teacher said to her in a whisper while clasping the girl's shoulders with long rough fingers. "Merna, you must never, never, I mean *never* mention the name of Troyan Stonovitch again or I can't say what might happen to you. This beating from old Maladic will seem like a little scolding in contrast to what could follow. When I was a girl I saw a woman hung up by her heels for nothing. For giving a German a drink of water."

"Giving a German a drink of water is nothing?" huffed one of the others, an older woman who had been standing quietly and taking it all in.

The matron began walking up and down now, twisting a little damp handkerchief in her fingers as she frowned and made her desperate plans aloud. She kept looking from the trembling Merna to the others who kept still and ready to hear her next words.

"Listen, Merna, we have been thinking how we must be very smart to get along now. We must be very clever and stick together. If we are not smart we might not live. It is that simple. You see that things are bad, girl, and they are getting worse. People are always looking for someone to blame, you understand that much, don't you? This is more serious than looking for firewood. "

"What? What do you want from me?" Merna asked, looking straight at her at last.

"We think you should marry Jorge," the mistress said. Then she was silent for a second. "We need you to start communications with him as soon as possible. As soon as your face is back to normal. The idea, of course, is to avoid any connection between your name and Troyan's. We must be smart."

The woman ran the damp handkerchief over her face and throat with an air of bitter exhaustion. She had once been very beautiful. Who knew what memories were flashing in her mind, or what other deals she had cut along the way.

"No," the girl shook her head. She was sitting on the edge of the bed now, with her face lowered and tears running down her cheeks. No. No. She did not want to marry. She did not want to marry me, Jorge Voinovitch. She kept shaking her head no. "No."

She must have resisted for days, but not more than that, for it was the same day the government sent in the gypsies and some musicians — organ grinders and fiddlers, terrible stuff, I recall — to play in the streets of the neighborhood to help the people forget the traitors, that I received the letter inviting me up to the orphanage to discuss the possibility of marriage with one Merna Louisa Voyic.

For several days I kept the letter and would pull it out of my boot, sometimes right in the street, and read it over, wondering if it was a joke or a trick of some kind being played on me. Nevertheless I let it be known I would at least come there, and on the appointed day I dressed in my new uniform and fine leather boots. Going into the military had been hateful to my soul, but I realized now how it had changed me. I had a proud look to my strong physique, and a certain arrogance in my step. But the best thing of all was my new Honda that floated like a piece of music up the long road under the arching elms. Like a piece of music.

It was a bike I had taken away from a U.N. Patrol Guard when I was in a town to the north. He was dumbfounded to have it jerked right out from under him, and he ran a few steps after me, then threw his hand in a little gesture of mockery as I rode off into the ramifying stone streets, laughing at him over my shoulder. A year ago it would have been unthinkable to me to do such a thing, but now it seemed permissible, a part of the times in which you could take what you were able to run with.

The first thing I saw on approaching the children's home was a great Serbian flag floating in the breeze outside the doorway. It made a great cracking noise each time the wind smacked it to and fro. I saluted it with vigor and clicked my heels, for you never can tell who might be watching.

Inside the doorway was a little cubbyhole of an entrance that smelled of promiscuous odors built up from so many years of children, sweetish whiffs of urine saturated with strong soaps and drifting unidentified scents, like in a hospital.

No one greeted me, although I rang the bell several times, but I was aware of a lot of activity in some classrooms just out of sight, children's voices reciting lessons, while others were apparently having meals in the basement area from the sound of the dishes and chatter.

Presently a blunt-faced matron in a white apron and large shoes made for a man came and showed me into a long hallway where, in a few minutes more, Merna Voyic herself and some of her guardians appeared and began to walk towards me across the bare, scrubbed wooden floor. My heart began to climb inside my chest as soon as I saw her. She looked as I last remembered her, but thinner, a slight girl really, with her fuzzy yellow hair hidden under a blue straw hat sprigged with a blossom of some sort. When she was quiet, close, I reached to take the hat away, but the matron's eyes jumped in her face and stared at me coldly, so instead we shook hands and bowed formally.

But my attention stayed straight on her, the single warmth that drew me. I raked my hand over my hair and stared into her eyes. There was more between us than anyone knew.

"Merna Voyic," I said to her as if she were the only one in the room, "no matter who or how many events bring two people together, there comes a time when their eyes must meet on their own accord. By their own wills."

I could tell she liked this kind of talk, and that she liked the change she saw in me. We stared into each other's faces, feeling the chaos between us. Slowly we began to smile. We would become friends, you could tell that. "Shall we?" the matron spoke again, this time more softly, and pointed out to the bricked court with the long field trails beyond, where we all walked and looked at the great countryside, which seemed a spacious, blooming, love-starved mountainous place.

Thank you to Matt Collinswood and Adrian Swain of the Kentucky Folk Art Center for the photo of *Nude With Hat.*